CLAIMING

His Wife

NIOMIE ROLAND

Claiming His Wife

Copyright © 2019 Niomie Roland

Books may be purchased in quantity and/or special sales by contacting the publisher, Niomie Roland, by email at alanasaunders_2011@hotmail.com.

Editing: Tanisha Stewart
www.tanishastewartauthor.com

First Edition

Published in the United States of America
by Niomie Roland

NIOMIE ROLAND

Dedication

To my mom who has always been my biggest supporter. From my first salty meal you said was the best food you've eaten and to always encouraging me to write despite my elementary school teachers' complaints about my essays being "too long."

NIOMIE ROLAND

Table of Contents

CLAIMING

His Wife

NIOMIE ROLAND

NIOMIE ROLAND

PROLOGUE

THE FAMILY MANSION SEEMED STRANGELY DEVOID of human presence.

Kalilah did not hear the usual hustle and bustle of the maids. Bates, her family's butler waved at her as he headed up the spiral staircase of her parent's mansion. It was a good thing, too, because she did not want to have an audience for what she was about to discuss with her father. In addition to that, she was sure she looked a mess. Her face was streaked with dried tears from all the crying she had been doing since she left Finn. *Finn.*

She thought about Finn, the love of her life, and took a deep breath. She remembered how she met him, and how everything changed for her. She didn't think that being in love was on the table at nineteen, but when she met Finn, she felt butterflies in her tummy. From their very first meeting, she'd known her life wouldn't be the same. She knew he was the one from their first magical kiss.

But she had been wrong about him. Wrong about everything she believed. Her life was now shattered. All the hopes and dreams she had for the two of them were now gone. She was here to put an end to the lies Finn told her before their relationship went any further. She raised her hand and knocked on her father's office door, and a voice from the other side beckoned her inside.

Entering her father's office, she saw that both her parents were present. Maybe this would be easier with her mom here. Her father Richard was seated at his desk and was the male version of his beautiful daughter Kalilah. He was tall and sturdy, and his sunken brown eyes and clean beard made him look even more handsome. As she walked into her father's office, she noted the scent of her father's expensive cologne in the air. His table was arranged neatly with files and his sleek personal computer.

Kalilah's mother, Katherine, sat on a chair opposite her husband and was dripped in gold, which further highlighted her caramel skin. Kalilah had inherited her mom's curly hair, which was currently hidden by the gold scarf that adorned her head. Mrs. Anderson's light brown eyes were focused on her manicure until her daughter walked in. Katherine was beautiful; she had a slender physique and could easily pass for a 30-year-old even though she was almost 50. She rearranged her loose blouse and crossed her legs as she faced her daughter.

"You look absolutely haggard, Kalilah. You know better than to be in such disarray. You're a reflection of your father and myself," her mom chastised. Kalilah opened her mouth to respond but her mom went on. "Have you thought about a location for the wedding reception?" Kalilah swallowed a sob. There would be no reception.

Kalilah cleared her throat and said, "I haven't, I…" Her father finally glanced up at her, and she was hastily interrupted by him.

"I was speaking to Finn earlier…" She knew all about their talk and how she was the prize to be traded. She had already spent all morning crying and she couldn't afford to let any more tears fall. Finn's betrayal shattered her very core.

"I know Father, and that's why…"

"Do not interrupt me, young woman, let me finish!" He bellowed as he fastened his vintage wristwatch on his wrist. "Finn told me that you wanted a small reception and I don't think that'll do."

She knew it was time to speak up, and so she did.

3

"Father I have something to say." Kalilah took a deep breath again, willing her tears to remain at bay. "I do not want a wedding at all. I no longer wish to marry Finn. It's over between us." After she said it, the picture of Finn's face when she had confronted him and broken up with him earlier came to mind, but she shrugged it away. She wouldn't allow herself to be fooled by him again. He'd seemed so surprised by the breakup, and had tried unsuccessfully to change her mind.

"What did you just say, girl?" Her father asked in a stern tone of voice. Kalilah shuddered where she stood.

"Father, please, let me explain!"

"Explain what? Did Finn raise his hand to you or take advantage of you?" Her mom asked finally chiming into the conversation.

He was a monster, but not that kind of monster.

"Of course not, Mother." How could she even think such a thing? Finn was capable of many things; lies and betrayal, yes, but not violence to a woman.

"So what's the issue?" Asked her father, who was looking at her intently.

Kalilah bit her lips, forgetting that she was wearing a matte lipstick. "I no longer wish to marry Finn or even be in a relationship with him. He used me to get ahead in your company and I am determined to not be anyone's pawn. He isn't who he claims to be."

Her father bellowed in laughter and swiveled in his chair. Kalilah didn't understand what was humorous about what she said.

When he was finally calm, he said, "You have no idea what you're talking about Kalilah," and then waved dismissively at her.

"Father, if you have any care for me, you will listen to me and allow me to make my own marital decisions. Please, Father," she pleaded, standing her ground, resolutely. She was cut off again.

"Do you not understand the importance of this union? What it means for the future of Anderson Realty? Our company must remain in this family. I am not about to let you ruin that over your silly whims, girl."

Kalilah flinched. If only he cared more about his daughters, and their feelings, more than his business.

She knew she had to forge ahead. She hoped that he saw her side of things.

"Marriage is for a lifetime, Father. It should be between two people who love and trust each other."

"Don't you love Finn? Weren't you gallivanting behind my back with him?"

"I was…"

Her father slammed his large hand on his desk. The action startled both women in the room and Kalilah took a step back.

"Calm down, darling," Katherine told her husband, and in return Richard placed a hand over his wife's. Her mom then turned to her and said, "Kalilah, you must do as your father says. He knows what's best for you."

"But Mother, I no longer wish to marry Finn. I broke up with him earlier," she pleaded, still hoping that this one time they would listen to her.

"Enough with this foolishness. I'll hear no more of this nonsense. Finn has an excellent business mindset and will make a fine husband. You will marry Finn, and Anderson Realty will remain in the family." Of course that was all he cared about; not her; never her. She fought the urge to roll her teary eyes.

"Why do you hate me, Father?" She asked in between sobs.

"If by hate you mean, sending you and your sister to private schools, allowing you both to travel the world and giving you unlimited access to all of my credit cards then yes. I suppose I hate you."

"Father please just listen to me. I won't marry Finn. I swear it on my life that I won't marry that user."

"Are you talking back to me girl? The audacity!" Her father barked.

"I'm so sorry Father, I didn't mean to talk back to you." Her tears formed a river down her cheeks.

"You forget your place, Kalilah. You will do as your father says," Katherine added placing your other hand on top of her husband's.

She mustered up her last bit of courage, raised her chin and said, "I won't do it and you can't force me to." She could barely recognize her own voice.

Her father looked toward his wife and then he looked in her direction as if surveying his prey. Kalilah knew instantly that her last bit of defiance was about to cost her dearly. And it was confirmed by her father's next words.

"Daughter, you have two options." He picked up his office phone and turned it in her direction.

"Call Finn now and tell him you made a mistake and you still wish to marry him, thereby securing our company's future - your future - or, you can kiss goodbye to every luxury I have afforded you and leave my house tonight with only the clothes on your back."

The ultimatum hit her hard. She gasped, losing her footing for a moment. Kalilah knew that tone, and she knew there was no use trying to convince her parents overwise. They had already made up their mind and dealt their final, painful card, and didn't care that she was a casualty in their ambitions.

She weighed the options placed before her by her father, and cringed as she thought of a way to get out of this predicament. Then, suddenly, she remembered the acceptance letter she received from the University of Washington a month ago, which she had chucked aside, and knew right away what she would do.

"What's your decision, Kalilah?" Katherine asked softly. If Kalilah didn't know better, she would mistake her mother's tone as compassionate, but she knew better. Her mother was incapable of empathy.

Kalilah's previous somber countenance faded as a summery smile spread across her face.

CHAPTER 1

THE POWERFUL ENGINE RUMBLED AT THE CURB as her driver made a slow turn and came to a stop. Kalilah took a deep breath. No time like the present to survey her surroundings. She had thought she was ready – she whipped herself into a frenzy of righteous purpose before she left the airport earlier. Her steely demeanor remained in place until she crossed the 520E highway from Dorval to Montréal and the feeling of coming home enveloped her.

The sway of familiar sights of French signs – the metro, Tim Horton's, and orange cones – brought back old memories. Who would have thought that she would have nostalgia to battle, in addition to the mission that brought her here? The 15-floor office building of Anderson Realty that she was now looking up at brought on the most reminiscent feelings. It stood strong, imposing, and blocking out the sun's rays with its magnificence. It was a testament to her failure... No, not failure.

To the great injustice that they had done her.

She was now back to finally put an end to the biggest mistake she'd ever made in her adult life. At twenty-five-years old and a recent graduate of the University of Washington in Seattle, Kalilah knew it was time to put an end the five-year façade. She was finally ready to live her own life in her own truth.

She breathed in the cool interior air of the car before her now steady hand reached for the door.

"Do I wait in the lobby for you, Miss?" her driver asked in his heavy Haitian accent. The kind gesture, however small, boosted her confidence.

"No, thank you, Owen, I will be but a minute," she assured him.

Kalilah had only met him earlier at the airport, and they had talked about quite a few things during the ride to downtown Montréal. She'd learned that he was originally from Haiti, and that he and his wife had moved to Quebec to join his wife's sister after the massive earthquake had hit the island years ago.

"Bonne chance, Madame," he replied and Kalilah sighed inwardly. Apparently, her inner consternation hadn't been missed. That wouldn't do; she had too much to fight for and she couldn't afford to hesitate or show weakness, especially to her ex-husband Finn. The slow burn of anger in her belly at the thought of him was a welcome sensation.

She had matured much over the years she was away.

Being alone in a new city, at twenty with no family to depend on for emotional support, had forced her to become self-reliant. It still rattled her mind just thinking about her growth, which had come during her college days majorly. She managed to emancipate herself from the chains of her past that held her back. The need for stepping out from under her parents' control had dawned upon her years ago, and she had ridden that wave gracefully and willfully. It was about time too, considering the circumstances under which she had left Montréal. She had to show that strength today in other to get what she came back for. She was no longer that lovesick puppy willing to believe that being in love solved all problems and that the world belonged to her.

Yanking open the taxi's door with an uncharacteristic defiance, she slid out the backseat and slammed the door shut behind her. Standing outside the car, the building was an even larger behemoth. Its hulking height was overpowering – it reminded her of the two men who had caused her life to be in such disarray. The building threatened to suck the steel right out of her soul; she wouldn't allow it. She was a woman on a mission.

Squaring her shoulders, Kalilah pushed forward. Putting one foot in front of the other would likely cost her dearly, but this was the only place she could come to get what she wanted. God help her and Finn, because she was determined to fully be free of them.

The lobby doors of Anderson Realty opened with a smooth hiss and the doorman bowed slightly at the waist as he ushered her in. Her heels clicked on the smooth, polished stone floors as she advanced toward the elevators. The large receptionist desk was empty. The understated opulence of the open space was an improvement over the last time she was here.

This new design was clean, bright, and airy. The stone was a perfect contrast to the textured walls and gold, stainless steel details. She took in the sparse furnishings, which consisted of five gold wire chairs covered with white sheepskin padding, strategically positioned around a glass coffee table situated in the center of the lobby. The last time she was here, the place was filled with grey carpet and dark walls. She turned from her survey of the room and stepped into the already open elevator. She pressed the familiar numbers of the floor where his office was located. When the elevator finally reached the 15th floor, she walked confidently toward a middle-aged Asian receptionist waiting with a patient smile. Kalilah couldn't remember this woman working here before she left.

She must be new, she thought.

"I am here to see Fi—Mr. Tremblay." She had almost said Finn, but had bitten her tongue. She wanted to keep this meeting as professional as possible.

The receptionist only inclined her head slightly as if she'd missed the almost faux pas.

"Do you have an appointment?"

Kalilah clenched her fist and then took a deep breath to calm herself. All week she had debated if she should book an appointment. One part of her thought it best, but the other part of her, that rebellious side she had discovered years ago when she had first met him – the person she loved most and was ready to do anything to be with – vehemently refused to give her enemies any warning before she struck.

Enemies? The thought struck something deep within her heart.

"Tell him it's Kalilah Anderson. He knows who I am," she replied, witnessing the receptionist widening her eyes.

"Of course, ma'am; please have a seat while I check if Mr. Tremblay is free."

Kalilah turned back to study the open room. Marble floors, glass walls, and subtle hints of gold scattered throughout the decor were a long way from the white walls, black trim, and tiled floors she remembered. Which reminded her, she needed to be nothing like that twenty-year-old girl who had cried herself to sleep for so many nights, wondering why she wasn't enough for him.

"Madame," the soft voice grabbed her attention and she turned toward the receptionist again,

"Please proceed to the very end of this hallway." She pointed to an area Kalilah had never seen before. "Mr. Tremblay's administrative assistant will be waiting for you." The choice of words brought a wry smile to her lips. *An administrative assistant and a receptionist – business must be booming!* she thought to herself.

The clicking of her heels filled the silence as she strode down the hallway. She passed several smaller offices until she came face to face with a stocky woman whose straight black hair was filled with grey strands. She regarded Kalilah with barely concealed curiosity.

"Madame Anderson?" she asked, her blue eyes brightening as she outstretched her hand.

Kalilah accepted the cool hands in hers and offered a small smile.

"Oui, c'est moi. Quel est votre nom?" She hadn't spoken the language in five years and was surprised by how quickly it came back to her.

"Please, call me Sabrina," she responded politely, in English, and then made a gesture with her hand. "Right this way. Mr. Tremblay is waiting for you. You're lucky to have come at this time, since he doesn't have any impending meetings."

Kalilah murmured something unintelligible under her breath at that snippet of information but didn't offer any response to Finn's assistant. She intended for this meeting to be short and quick.

After thanking Sabrina for walking her to Finn's office door, she raised her hand slowly and knocked. Why did she knock? Old habits die hard. It was something that was ingrained into her when her father was in his office. It gave too much power to that room, to her past.

"Come in!" A male voice sounded through the door.

***

In the five years of heading this company, Finn could admit that he had never waited for an appointment with bated breath before today. The call from his assistant stating that Kalilah Anderson was here to see him had shattered his morning, like cold water coming into contact with a hot glass. Instantly feeling a trickle of sweat on his nape, anger suddenly replaced a heady feeling. *Anger is better*, he told himself. It afforded him a level of control. At least that was something he could manage – controlling his emotions came easy because of his line of work.

In business, it was dangerous to allow your opponents to see you sweat.

Rebranding the company and pushing it to even greater heights had taken up a chunk of his time. Working 14- to 16-hour days helped him forget the mess he had called his life. The truth was that he had been running. The worst part about the entire fiasco was that he wasn't guilty of anything Kalilah accused him of or believed him to be. He still didn't understand how things had gotten so out of hand between them. He blamed himself for the chasm that now separated them. He took full responsibility for that. He should've tried harder to tell her the truth. Now, she was on her way to his office, and he didn't know what to think.

The knock on his office door further destabilized him. His spine stiffened. He masked his emotions before saying, "Come on in!" He hoped his voice sounded more confident than he felt. He rose from his chair and walked across to the glass wall which overlooked downtown Montréal. His eyes were accosted by a view he couldn't appreciate in that moment. He had known from the moment she left Seattle and had received a call the moment her flight had landed in the

Canada, yet he felt unprepared to meet her. He never expected to be her first stop. He would be lying to himself if he didn't admit to hoping that she had returned to finally settle down here – with him.

The door swung open and he turned to look her over.

Cool dark eyes latched onto his own dark blue ones from across the room. There wasn't a hint of kindness in her eyes. Her face was neutral but her body language seemed combative. Despite her currently hostile demeanor, she was still the most beautiful woman he'd ever seen, and he had told her such countless times in the past. High cheekbones, which he had kissed countless times, smooth umber skin that he tasted whenever they were alone, and a slender physique that his hands used to roam. He groaned at his thoughts. He also noticed that she'd grown into her curves. Her breasts were fuller and her hips were wider. He felt the rush of blood to his manhood, so he quickly brought his eyes back to her cool glare.

That unrelenting stare could douse the flames to even the most ferocious fire.

Finn clenched his jaw and steadied his breathing before saying, "Hello Lilah."

"Hello Finn." Her breathy voice crossed the air to hit him in the gut with a savage blow. Five years was a long time.

"You look beautiful as always. Finally came back to take your place as my wife?" He asked this in French.

"I want an annulment," her words fell upon him quickly, cutting off all rational thought. He was not proud of losing control but it was too late for apologies when a red haze of anger clouded his vision and primal urges surged through him. *Mine.*

"Did you hear me?" Kalilah repeated.

CHAPTER 2

KALILAH WATCHED FINN CLENCH HIS FISTS and release them intermittently. The veins in his neck looked ready to pop. He parted his lips and clamped them shut again in as many seconds. His brows slowly slumped in the middle and rose at their ends. Unbothered by the anger she knew was currently overtaking him, Kalilah remained firm in her stance and crossed her arms over her chest. He was struggling, no doubt, and she wondered what exactly he seemed to be battling with.

"Did you hear what I said?" she inquired, hoping to spark some response from the man. Why did he have to be so good looking?

"Close the door and come in, Lilah, unless you need the protection that it offers." He finally broke out his words, challenging her.

"My name is Kalilah." Head tilted high, she slammed the door using her foot and stalked further into his office. *Challenge accepted.* "I want an annulment Finn."

"I heard you the first time," he bit out.

"And?"

"Not happening," he replied bluntly as his tone of voice turned from thunderous to mischievous. She noticed him unclench his fists as his six-foot-four-inch frame confidently stalked closer.

Kalilah knew what the look meant, even if it had been a long time since she saw it.

"Please, Finn; I am not here for your games or manipulations."

"What are you here for then?" The innuendo was obvious, and it grated on her skin.

In a twist, she found herself both enraged and trapped in his handsome snare, which was becoming more apparent the longer she gawked at him. His perfectly chiseled jawline and neatly aligned teeth glared right back at her. She centered her gaze on his lips, and memories of him kissing her tortured her mind. She remembered how much she longed for them. The familiar scent of his cologne played havoc on her senses. Its effects on her hadn't subsided; if anything, it made her more aware of him.

It wasn't her damn fault that the man was annoying and attractive in equal measure. Something was different about his appearance, but she just couldn't figure out what. Then she figured it out. It was his hair. She noticed it when she studied his haircut, now a faded crewcut, way shorter than it used to be. It didn't take away from his raw masculinity.

She could almost see his muscles through his designer suit. *Why did he have to look so good?* Why couldn't he have had a potbelly? Why the heck was she getting turned on by just looking at him? It wasn't her fault that the ghost and dreams of her eighteen-year-old self was haunting her in full vengeance. She knew the vein in her throat was pulsing; hell, her entire body was vibrating with barely suppressed anger and something else…

Desire? Need? She would ignore that for now. She would feed off the anger that came every time she thought of his betrayal. Anger made her remember the pain, but would her anger stop Finn Tremblay? From the look of determination on his face, she guessed not.

Kalilah took a step back to gather her composure before she fixed her eyes on him again. She didn't have time for this, or for whatever else the past was trying to drag back into her consciousness. She had to remember Jonathan. Her future with Jonathan was the reason she had to stand against all the bullies in her life, starting with this one.

"I said I want an annulment," she repeated, and it felt like she was talking to an idiot.

"And I said I have no interest in dissolving this union," he replied in the same dispassionate tone.

"You can't stop it," she replied easily. "There is no reason to drag this on any further."

"But I already have," he returned with just enough mockery to sting. She felt as if she was a kid again, being toyed with. A child who was about to be denied something because of sheer adult perversity. Well, she was all grown up now, and the word 'no' didn't scare her anymore; in fact, it made her work twice as hard to get what she wanted.

The calm words inflamed her even more.

"This is my life!" Kalilah started and took several deep steadying breaths to rein in her seething temper. "My life, not some company merger or some other office decision you have final say on. I want to be free."

Finn winced at that, and it prompted her to savor her victory, no matter how little and brief it might be.

"Free? You've always been free. Free enough stay away for five years and waltz back here demanding the impossible."

"You don't understand," she returned coolly and rather oddly as she heard herself.

"Then make me. I tried for almost one year after you left me to tell you my side of things and to make things right between us, but you refuted every effort I made," he said resolutely as he turned back to the view.

The switch in his tone struck her in awe and caused her to mellow in resolve. She bit back her previously composed words and gulped them down in a hot, choking manner.

"I met someone else and he proposed to me. I can't accept his proposal until this is settled between us," she explained, ignoring everything else he had said. She wasn't interested in revisiting the past. Whatever happened, happened, and there was nothing that could be done to change it. Nothing she wanted to do to change it either.

She saw his body freeze, and his hands formed fists. He then turned toward her slowly and she could see the frown across his forehead. She thought she saw pain in his eyes as well, but that couldn't be possible. There was no reason for him to be pained. Her revelation, no doubt, was shocking and had caught him off guard. She took his stunned silence as the perfect opportunity to continue her argument.

"I care for him deeply."

"Do you love this man?"

"Yes, I do. Very much."

"Okay, you love him. But are you in love with him?"

The question took her by surprise. How could she explain what she felt toward Jon? She didn't love him with that all-encompassing passion she had felt toward Finn, but she did love him in a way that was sobering. She could actually think when she was around Jon, which was refreshing. With Finn, it was all about feeling. He was her drug and she was always high. He made her feel like she could conquer anything that she wanted to and that the world belonged to her. She also realized that when you love someone so strongly, the heartbreak is ten times worse. She never wanted to feel that kind of heartbreak again.

"I don't owe you any explanation," she said finally.

He continued his intent study of her face, and the air in the room felt thinner. She felt uncomfortable under his microscopic stare.

"So, not only do you slink back into town after four years of pretending I didn't exist, you returned solely to collect what you need to go back into your faithless love nest? How dare you stand in front of me and demand I give you an annulment," he said incredulously, and then took a step toward her. She stood there, unable to move, surprised by his outburst. "We are married, Kalilah, not acquaintances. Doesn't the sacredness of the union give you pause? Have you thought thoroughly about what you're asking of me?"

Despite his obvious anger, she didn't think he would become violent toward her. She knew he would never hurt her, not physically at least. She leveled her stare and responded with as much assertion as she could muster.

"This union has been anything but sacred. I don't know about you but I'm ready to break free from this farce. And yes, I have thought about this. I gave it five full years of thought. Now, thanks to the genuine love Jonathan has afforded me, I finally have a reason to end this marriage and I don't give two shits if you don't like it," she countered, her pulse pumping with barely suppressed outrage. How dare he lay the blame at her feet?

"So you think our relationship was meaningless? A lie?" he ground out; his piercing blue stare was fixated on her.

"Yes," she responded, "and at everyone's directing, I played my part to the very hilt. Now I'm done. Allow me to live my life and be happy with someone who loves me."

"You can't possibly believe that our plans and what we shared weren't real? I loved you and you loved me. It was me and you against the world. We made vows to love each other forever, and now you want an annulment from me, so you can marry a man you're not even in love with?"

Her lips parted to respond but he cut her off.

"Don't you dare lie to me about your feelings toward this man."

She snapped her mouth shut. *Let him think what he wants,* she thought. She didn't want to think about those girly fantasies and promises either. That naïve girl had disappeared a long time ago, along with those hopes and dreams.

She was relieved when he turned. *Good.* He must have realized that she meant what she said.

"Tell me about this bastard who wants to come between a man and his wife." He said 'wife' possessively and turned to face her again, his voice tight.

It broke her heart that what he mourned was not her; he probably saw all his ambitious dreams slipping away. *I don't care,* she said repeatedly in her mind. No matter how much she said it though, it didn't stop the bruise on her heart from widening.

"He isn't a bastard," she snapped. "He is twice the man you'll ever be and I can't wait to be his." She was deliberately being vindictive, to hurt him how he had hurt her, and she suspected she didn't miss her mark. His face turned a stony mask at her declaration. His blue pools turned darker and colder than she had ever seen them.

"No matter how much you deny it, the truth remains that you are my wife, and that's how it's going to remain."

"It's hardly been a marriage, and besides – it hasn't been consummated," she replied noncommittally. She cursed inwardly for bringing their sex life (or lack thereof) into the mix.

"That's my fault." His words sounded weak and she knew what he was implying.

When they had started dating, years before, he didn't do much more than kiss her. He claimed it was because she was much younger than him, and because she was his boss's daughter and he didn't want to cross a line that they'd never be able to uncross. At the time, he was twenty-five and she was nineteen. She had fallen head over heels for him. She had tried to seduce him many times, but he always refuted her advancements at the last minute. She believed that to be one of the two reasons he'd proposed to her six months after they'd started dating. He had fooled her into believing that he had wanted to do things the "right" way with her. But now she knew better. He was only using her to get promoted within the company, without doing anything that may hurt his chances. Not that anything would; her father would've sold her off to him anyway.

"And I'm willing to fix that issue immediately if you so wish." Finn's words jolted her from her runaway thoughts. "We can go home," he said in an exuberant tone. "After all, it is your home as well, and I am a gentleman and will not make any unwanted moves until you ask me to. It'll be an interlude to erase all others."

Kalilah caught the emotion laced in his voice, and she swallowed before she responded. Her body was heated; not from anger, but from erotic images of how she would feel in his strong arms. She found it very unsettling, so she swallowed, blinking when she suddenly remembered the times they hid away, trying to keep their relationship from being discovered by her parents. They had taken pleasure in discovering the passions found in different types of kisses.

Vexed by the images that were trying to betray her will, she blurted out, "An oversight for which I am now grateful. Now release me from this farce you call a marriage."

"Forget it." The hopeful look was gone. The stony-faced capitalist was back.

"Oh, no you don't! You married me to get this company and now you have it. I'm happy that one of us got what they wanted out of life, Mister Chief Operating Officer, but now it's my turn now," she pronounced firmly. "I have never asked you for anything, and I don't need anything else from you. Get your lawyer to contact mine and sign the papers." Under Quebec law, a marriage that was contracted by force is eligible for an annulment. She felt proud of herself. Before coming back to Montréal, she'd stayed up every night for the past month doing her research on divorce proceedings when she realized that her marriage was eligible for an annulment instead.

Her lawyer agreed.

"I didn't get everything that I wanted," Finn replied. "Do you know what I really want, still want?" The calm man was now back in control.

But Kalilah was a woman on a mission.

"I don't care about what you want. Give me the one thing I want, the only thing I'll ever need from you."

"You're asking for a lot – too much. I can't do it," he said as if the decision was final. He said the most unreasonable things in that logical tone and she wanted nothing more than to slap the calmness from his handsome face.

"Finn Tremblay!" Her control shot to pieces at his constant rebuffs. Her heart had begun to ram hard against her ribcage and her knees threatened to fail her.

"Yes, Mrs. Tremblay." His mocking smile was now back in place. She would never be able to take his name as long as they lived here. Women in Quebec were not able to take their husband's last name, and he knew that. She thought of how desperately she had wanted his name when they first spoke of marriage. She couldn't believe how naïve she'd been to believe they'd live happily ever after. She had her father's name and she didn't think it was a better choice either. It was the worst choice. It served to remind her that she was all by herself. Alone. Single, although married – for now.

"My name is Kalilah Anderson." She gritted her teeth. "Enough with your schemes. Just agree to the annulment so that we can both move on with our lives. We both know that the only reason you're saying no is because I'm the one who wants this annulment."

"Schemes?"

It was obvious that he liked toying with her, enjoyed her acute discomfort and would continue to say no until kingdom come just because he had the power to do just that.

"I didn't stutter, did I?"

"I see," he returned.

"Do you really?" She countered in a brisk tone.

"I assure you that I do."

"Will you give me what I want?" The words were out before she realized how loaded it was with double innuendoes. And he caught it, his eyes flickering indication. "We can't continue as we've been doing."

"What exactly do you want?" he asked suggestively totally ignoring her last sentence.

"Keep your frat house humor to yourself. I have already told you want I want," she demanded. She was beginning to get annoyed. It felt like they were going around in circles.

"I won't," he returned lightly.

A rush of anger evaporated her good sense and she raised her hand to smack him. His eyes widened with astonishment. She brought her hand back down to her sides. She could feel the anger swell her chest, so she closed her eyes and counted to ten while taking deep steady breaths. She couldn't afford to lose her calm at this point. She couldn't afford to give him the upper hand. Her future was more important than her moment's anger.

She opened her eyes and focused her dispassionate glare at him.

They faced each other across the cool expanse and waited for one to yield.

"I see that more than your need to be free, has awoken. I can't remember you being this fiery," he commented in a voice that didn't even begin to hide the amusement he felt.

"I have you to thank for that."

"You look even more radiant when you're angry. I like it."

"You've got me confused with someone who cares about your opinion," she huffed. "I am completely unaffected by what you say or do."

"Care to test out those words?" The husky tone seized more than her voice, as he caught her hands and trapped her body against the wall.

"Let me go," she bit out. He brushed his fingers gently down her face as if trying to draw a portrait of her in his mind.

Kalilah squirmed. Each touch seemed to chip away at the wall she had built between them. He paused, his finger above her lip and all she could think about was kissing him.

"So soon? And here I thought you weren't affected by what I said." He then leaned in until the words were whispered into her ear. "Or did." The feel of his breath against her skin set her nerves on fire and activated her sleeping limbs. He gently brought her palms up against the wall and over her head and them placed his larger palms over hers. She stiffened for a moment but relaxed her palms underneath his. No words were said. He gazed down at her intensely and she knew that look. She felt nineteen again. She had seen this look many times right before he claimed her lips. *And damn!* It still affected her. She needed to get away from him and his strength and his cologne that brought up memories she wanted buried. She began to struggle against him. Her movements did the opposite of what they were meant to. Her body rubbed against his and instead of wanting an escape, she wanted to feel more of him. She wanted him to kiss her. She felt his manhood spring to life against her thigh.

"Kalilah, you really shouldn't…" he warned, his voice sounding strained, wavering, then breaking the temporary spell she was under.

"Let me go," her tone panicked.

"But I love your current disposition," he returned.

"Crowded?" Her voice sounded breathy.

"No, under my control." He must have realized the moment the words left his mouth that they were the exact wrong words to say, because he leaned away from her a bit.

"Let go of me this minute!" Her voice was icy and dismissive. He took his time releasing her from his hold and then walked around to his desk and sat in his chair. Kalilah tried to ignore his presence as she fiddled with the button on her floral blouse.

"I didn't mean it that way," he said.

She disregarded him and brushed a loose strand of hair from her face. *Under my control.* Not anymore. She was grateful for those words; they had jolted her back to reality. God knows that one more second with her body besieged by Finn's against the wall and she would've given in to the intense lust she felt. It terrified her that she had never gotten to this height of intimacy with Jonathan, and yet here she was all over Finn. She groaned internally; this wasn't how she planned this meeting to go. So much for making progress. What a waste of time! She should've known better than to show up at her ex-husband's office and expect things to go as smoothly as she planned. She let out a slow breath and tugged at the hem of her floral blouse once more before marching to the door. She had to escape and regroup before she made a fool of herself.

"I'll give you what you want." Those words stopped her in her tracks.

She whirled her head toward him, her dark eyes widened, mouth agape as if she'd lost her hearing. She searched his face for any hint of amusement. His stony mask gave nothing away. *Did he finally accept things were over?* Hope bubbled in her chest.

"On one condition only," he added and that's all it took to shatter her hope in its entirety.

She glared at him speculatively.

"Look, I don't know what game you're playing, but I'll not be a party to it. I'm asking for what I know you surely want as well. We both need to move on with our lives."

He winced at her declaration, and this time she didn't get any satisfaction from his torment. She had no idea why he was hesitant to get the annulment. She doubted he ever loved her. Theirs wasn't a story with a happy ending. He probably wanted to stay married for his stake in the company. Her heart sank at the thought. She didn't know why the belief that he only wanted to stay married for the sake of finally becoming CEO of company wounded her heart.

The silence thickened between them until she broke eye contact and turned away.

"Please wait." Despite her annoyance she found herself turning to look at him. That position suited him. Lord of all, at the very peak of his ambitions. *God, why did he have to be so handsome?* "My only condition is that you allow me to date you for three months. If you still feel the same way about marriage," he explained calmly, his unwavering stare fixed on her, "By the end of that time frame, then I'll sign whatever papers you want me to."

Regardless of the physical and emotional distance between them, her body trembled as she felt the temperature rise an extra ten degrees. Overwhelmed she blinked to ward off any unwelcome thoughts in her mind.

She realized she was still staring blankly at him when she noticed his arched brow. Finding it hard to look away, she felt like her body was held captive under his intense scrutiny. She had forgotten how his eyes could pin her like a laser and saw right through her soul. *Fucking power moves.*

"Is this a joke? Are you playing some kind of game with me?"

"Who, me?" He asked with amplified innocence. "Never."

"Why three months?" She found the timeline a bit strange.

"It doesn't matter."

Strange. Very strange.

"So why go through all this? I am confident that I will not change my mind. A few dinners here and there won't change the way I feel and my abhorrence towards you."

"You sure about that?" His tone was cocky now.

"Yes. I've never been surer of anything in my life. Finn, I won't ever forgive or forget your deception." Her chest tightened, tears threatened, but she was not going to break down in front of him. That would be a sign of weakness. She truly felt like they were meant to be once upon a time. But all he wanted was a place in her father's company.

"Give me a chance to disprove everything you think you know about me. If by the end of the three months your mind hasn't wavered about me, I'll give you your annulment without a fight." He added quickly.

An uncomplicated annulment was a dream she didn't dare have. It seemed too easy to ascertain. Finn seemed too confident in his position.

"If you decline my offer and move forward with your immediate plans, I will oppose this annulment at every turn. Since you've been gone, I've acquired way more assets, and your name is on everything I've acquired. I will have my lawyer bury yours in paperwork for the next several years over the division of property."

The coldness in his voice caused a shiver to her spine and she knew he meant every word. Between both of their assets they could be stuck in court forever since they didn't have a prenup to begin with. She had refused to sign the documents her father had presented to Finn and herself. One of her final acts of rebellion against her father. She studied for a moment longer as her mind battled between emotions and thinking over possible loopholes in his plan. She knew too much to trust him. Men like him and men like her father should never be underestimated. She would agree with his deal and in three months, she was certain things would be over and done with. She figured the months would roll by fast. She finally gave him a slow nod then turned around to leave.

"I need verbal confirmation, Kalilah."

She rolled her eyes.

"I accept the offer, Finn, but just so you know, I'll never change my mind. Not about this." She jerked the door and without a backward glance stepped through it.

"Not if I can help it." he returned under his breath and she heard him clear across the hall. His cockiness riled her up and strengthened her resolve to play his game and win.

She couldn't resist having the final word.

"Game on," she yelled confidently. She would teach him a valuable lesson indeed. If he thought that his power games would work on her, he had something coming. Kalilah almost strutted out of the building with a kind of elegance she didn't feel. She inclined her head briefly as she passed by the administrative assistant and again to the receptionist at the lobby desk on the ground floor. The doorman wished her a good day and she rewarded him with a half-smile before heading toward the car where her driver Owen was patiently waiting for her.

CHAPTER 3

THE MOMENT KALILAH CLEARED THE DOOR, Finn took a few slow breaths to regroup and refocus. She was the only person that could blow his focus to pieces, and five years had not dulled her potency. He missed her. He was shocked and proud of the assertiveness he'd seen her display today. She was now a woman willing to meet her battles head on. He admired that and it turned him on to no end. He loosened his tie and shifted uncomfortably in his seat.

When she had cocked her hip in the face of his mockery, clenched her fists and demanded her freedom, he almost couldn't hear her words over the roar of blood in his ears. A fierce arousal that had threatened to undo him had fired his loins. She wasn't even aware of how much power she had over him. He would do anything for her; he had given her the break she had coldly requested years ago.

"I need you to leave my apartment now." Her tone had held no emotion. Her eyes had glistened with tears, her dark skin dull. He had tried to cut in but she had continued. "I don't want to hear anything else you may have to say right now. You've hurt me enough, and I need this time away from you. Being around you hurts my very soul. Please leave."

He had left her apartment then, and promised to give her all the time she needed until she felt ready to listen to him. He had vowed to wait for her, for as long as she needed to sort through her emotions. Every well-laid plan he had ever made in his life, for himself, for their marriage, came tumbling down like King's Landing. And it hurt, dammit, it hurt immensely – but her absence hurt more. Her refusal to speak with him or believe him had hurt him so much. She returned every gift he had sent and refused to even speak to him on the three occasions he showed up in Seattle. The only time she showed was to tell him that she needed more time. He decided to pull back and give her some space. The truth was, he'd taken the coward's way out. He wanted to flee the keen disappointment he saw in her eyes every time he visited her. He finally resigned himself to waiting until she was ready to hear him out.

Letting her go all those years ago had been the worst decision he'd ever made. He'd poured the rest of his soul into the company he'd gotten from her sacrifice; their sacrifice. Over the last few years he became a workaholic, gradually taking on more and more responsibility in the business. Assisting everyone he could within the company, so he could learn how everything worked. He even assisted his father-in-law with some of the duties he had as CEO. He loved the challenge because now he knew the business like the back of his hand. Thankfully, his hard work had paid off, because now he was the chief operating officer, and their profits were higher than ever. People assumed he was given the position because of his relationship with Kalilah, but he earned this position. He knew the job of the janitor up to the CEO. The goal was to eventually take over for his father-in-law after he retired. Unfortunately, placing his full attention on work came with its disadvantages. There was nothing for him to look forward to except closing huge deals.

The years following Kalilah's departure were filled with dreadful weekdays and equally bleak weekends. Now she was back, and her return opened a floodgate of emotions that were almost forgotten. He had hoped that her return would be different; a gentle reunion of sorts where they would talk through everything that had happened in the past, but he could not have been any further from the truth.

"I promise you, Finn, nothing will ever come between us. You're everything to me." She would tell him this every time they parted back then. Her eyes held so much hope. He had taken her proclamation seriously because he felt the same way about her. Those promises had dissipated, along with the girl who shared those declarations. For the past five years he had loved her, and for five years he had counted on her youthful promises of unconditional love to bridge the gap when she was ready to fully listen to him and settle down with him. He now realized that was naïve of him to rely on her promises. She was no longer a girl. She was now a woman, and unfortunately, not his woman. He had waited too long; here she was, irate, beautiful, all grown up and wanting nothing he had to offer except his acquiescence to an annulment.

His heart was doomed; he knew it from the moment she walked into his office. The resentment he had felt toward her long ago for not giving him a chance to explain his side of the story had dissipated. When he pinned her against the wall, her floral scent gripped his senses, and it took all the self-control he'd learned over the years not to give in to the primitive urges surging through him. He wanted one taste of her plump lips. She was so close, yet so far away; she looked so alluring, and the challenge she presented aroused him more if that was possible. When she started bucking under him, he had to clench his teeth to keep in the groan that her unintentionally provocative actions drew from him.

He had released his wildcat before she thwarted his advances further. He wondered how things might have turned out had she believed in him and his love for her. They probably would have had a child or two by now. *Would their kids have her curly hair?* A smile curved his lips at the thought, but it was short-lived when another thought came to mind. The sacrifices he had made both physically and emotionally; contrary to what he was sure others in her position might believe, he hadn't looked at another woman ever in the years since Lilah left. He'd had a few dates to social events, and even though some of the women were willing and open to a one-night stand, his pledge to his wife and the need to see it through regardless of the distance prevented him from ever being unfaithful. After a five-year drought, he was ready to swim in the river of her most coveted heat.

His blood heated with anger at the thought of her replacing him. *Who was this man? What did he do for a living? Was he an American?* Questions roamed his mind, questions he needed answered, but there was no use. It would be naïve to dismiss this other man, even though she couldn't admit to being in love with him. He was certain that the man, whatever his name was, was a threat to their reconciliation for the simple fact that she returned to town only for the dissolution of their union. The urge to find this man and kick the shit out of him was high, but that wouldn't go over well with Kalilah. Besides, he may not even know about her marriage.

He quickly shook off that bitter thought. Kalilah was honest to a fault, and she would have told this man about her marriage. Actually, citing how much she had changed, it was a genuine possibility that this jerk didn't even know what he'd gotten himself into. Suddenly, he had this unsettling image of a stranger exploring his wife's body and doing things that he had yet to do with her. What were his intentions, he wondered – perhaps he knew of her huge trust fund, and wanted to sink his hooks into it (not that Kalilah wasn't capable of enticing a man who was fully invested in who she was as a person). At his uncomfortable thoughts, his heart felt like it was being ripped out of his chest. He didn't want to lose her, not now and definitely not for a second time.

He swiveled his office chair to face the tall windows overlooking downtown Montréal. People could also assume that he had married her for money and position.

He had met his father-in-law, Richard, when he interned at the company eight years ago, after gaining his master's degree in business from McGill University. He was twenty-six at the time, fresh out of university with something to prove to the world. He got to work early and left late, and he wasn't shy about asking questions either. After all, how could he learn if he never asked any questions? He interned there a full three months before meeting Richard Anderson, CEO of Anderson Property Group.

When he first met Richard, he'd boldly asked him in the lobby of the offices why a business of such good standing wasn't offering franchise services, as it would improve valuations and thereby boost growth and improve profits. Richard regarded him intently for a long time that day, until finally he invited him to his office and picked his brain about the other ideas he thought would be good for the company.

Finn had made suggestions about their website and how it could be improved to offer people a virtual experience of real estate. Thanks to Finn and his never-ending questions the company also now offered franchise opportunities and protection services for home buyers and sellers. Richard had hired him on the spot, and invited him to dinner with his family. That was the first time he'd met Kalilah. She'd peeked at him throughout dinner under the cover of her thick lashes. He'd ignored it. She'd looked no older than sixteen, and he wasn't trying to go to jail. In addition to that, he'd only just landed his first job, and messing with the boss's daughter was not a good idea. His interest piqued, however, when she mentioned her upcoming graduation from CEGEP. He had asked her age then, and found out that she had just turned nineteen.

He was immediately put off by the age difference between them. He considered her a child, but he was drawn to her like a moth to a flame. After that first dinner, he frequented the Anderson mansion numerous times for dinner and other soirees. During those months, he got to know Kalilah more, and he realized that even though she appeared younger than her age, she was no child. She was mature, intelligent, and sexy. Everything about her deepened his attraction. She knew what she wanted out of life, and had a passion for helping others and trying out new adventures. She was devoted to everything that she did, including loving him. She would listen to him vent his frustrations about everything happening at work, and in return he would listen to her vent her frustrations about school and her parents. They made a wonderful team, and she quickly became his best friend. The best friend he was in love with.

Memories of the first night their friendship shifted to something more rushed through his mind.

They had been at one of her family dinners, and she and her mother got into another disagreement about what her university major would be. She had walked out of the dining room and stormed from the house. Finn had no idea what compelled him to hurry after her, but he had. He quickly excused himself from dinner and followed her. He found her seated under the dark gazebo on the back lawn, sobbing. Her obvious anguish crushed his heart, and so he had brushed a tear from her cheek and held her against his broad chest as he rubbed her back. Her face was pressed to his chest while he reassured her that everything would be okay. His body had reacted immediately to her being in his arms. He had ignored it. He had held her like that for what seemed like hours, but it was merely minutes.

Her sobs had gradually subsided, and she had looked up at him then. He couldn't see her face clearly in the darkness, but he imagined her eyes still filled with unshed tears. She had brought her face up closer and pressed her lips to his. It was gentle at first, unsure. But the feel of her lips upon his had opened a floodgate of desire, and he had deepened the kiss. His tongue had coaxed her lips open and began an exploration of her mouth. His hand travelled from her back and cupped her ass, bringing her body even closer to his. When they'd broken apart, he was in disbelief of what he'd just done, but Kalilah was smiling.

That was their first kiss, and many had followed. After that night, theirs became a relationship of stolen minutes, in the shadows of the mansion, to make out and spend time together. He would pick her up from school on days he got off early, and bring her to the old port or Mont Royal. They went to the movies, clubs, and dinner together. One weekend they even drove to Ottawa to meet his family.

"You'll never move here now, will you?" His mom laughed gleefully. He knew what she meant. His family had lived in Montréal before moving to Ottawa, where his stepfather opened up more of his fast food franchises. The plan had always been for him to finish school in Montréal and then join them.

"What do you mean?" He feigned ignorance.

"I'm your mother and I know you. I see how you look at Kalilah. You won't leave her." His mom's conclusions were true. He had no plans to move to Ottawa while Kalilah lived in Montréal.

"I love her, Mom," he had confessed. She had smiled and cupped his face, and told him to take good care of Kalilah. He readily agreed, knowing that she meant more to him than the air he breathed.

That trip had been difficult for him as well; he abstained from having sex with Kalilah, but she didn't make it easy for him. The little minx had enticed him with her movements and skimpy outfits. All they had cared about was each other. His desire to claim her fully kept mounting, and he decided that he would ask her to be his wife. Before he even got to it, Richard had cornered him and asked him about his interest in his daughter.

"I know you're seeing my daughter," Richard said matter-of-factly, while they were in his office discussing their latest condo development. Finn was surprised. He and Kalilah had tried very hard to keep their relationship under wraps, and apart from Kaiya – Kalilah's younger sister – no one else knew. But what was also surprising to him, was that he didn't feel fear that Richard knew they were together. He didn't care who knew. He loved Kalilah and he would be with her, even if it meant losing his job.

"I love your daughter with my entire being, and I intend to propose to her soon. I apologize for dating her behind your back, but I won't ever apologize for loving her or wanting to make her my wife. If you want to fire…" Richard cut him off.

"I started this company years ago as a means to support my family and elevate our position in this country and in the world." Finn was unsure of where the conversation was headed but he listened. "As you know, I'm getting older, and I have two daughters who show little interest in this company; one is only interested in making the world a happier place through dance, and the other only wants to help every lost soul she comes across," the man scoffed, and Finn sat there patiently, attentively waiting for the older man to make his point, "and it would be such a waste if this company didn't remain in the hands of family…"

Before he knew it, Richard had cajoled him into proposing sooner that he'd planned and offered to promote him to the COO Chief Operating Officer position of the company on the day after the wedding. He figured since he'd already planned to ask for her hand in marriage, that it didn't matter when he proposed, or what her father did. He saw it solely as a means to provide for them after they got married.

No, they were not the same; he had married the woman he cared deeply about. One touch from her and he was set ablaze. He got the position in the company as an added bonus, not that she saw it that way or would see it that way. She believed he played her to get what he wanted.

"Tabarnak," he muttered to himself.

She had overheard the end of his conversation with her father. He saw the look of betrayal on her face and the tears that glistened in her eyes the moment he had left her father's home office. Finn tried to explain to her, but the cold stare she fixed on him made him regret ever having that conversation. Finn turned his chair towards his desk again and picked up his cellphone. He needed information and he knew just the man for the job.

"Hey, Lucien." His voice was deliberately upbeat for the benefit of his friend.

"Hey, Chief," his friend of twelve years thundered down the phone.

Lucien had been a special unit army member until he had retired to open his own private investigations business. It had taken off with a bang, even if he bitched on the amount of spousal cheating cases he had to pursue daily.

"You've not forgotten my name have you?" Finn called out.

"When pigs fly!" Came the loud retort over the phone.

They talked a bit more about what had been happening in their lives, until Finn told him about Kalilah and the ridiculous demands she placed on him.

"That burns; you want me to come over?" The offer of support shored him up just enough to go on.

"No, but I need something from you."

"Anything."

"I want everything you can find on this guy Kalilah has been dating. I don't remember his name anymore but I'm sure that's not going to prevent you from getting results," he flattered.

"His name is Jonathan, and I know when you're buttering me up."

The shock seized his vocal cords for a few seconds before he blurted out.

"How did you know?"

"Currently on his Facebook page and he has many pictures of the two of them on his page, but she doesn't have any of him on hers. Looks like she barely posts anything," Lucien informed him in a preoccupied voice.

"Facebook?"

"For a multimillionaire, you're so behind the times; you're prehistoric." Sound of keys tapping in the background filled the line.

"I know what Facebook is," Finn ground out.

"Congratulations. So, all the information on one Jonathan Sawyer coming up. If it helps, he looks like a wimp." Lucien informed him.

Just what I need, my wife being taken away by a wimp, he thought.

"And Finn," Lucien called out.

"Yeah?"

"This one is all on me," he offered. "I know how it was when she left town and I know it hasn't been easy."

"Thanks, man." To reject the offer would be an insult, Lucien was not overly emotional, no doubt a by-product of the upbringing he had from his soldier father.

"Catch you later," he called over the phone and Finn dropped the call.

"I cannot lose her again," he declared to himself a while later. He needed to make a foolproof plan to sweep her off her feet and have her head spinning so fast that she would not even remember the name of the man she claimed to love. He needed to remind her why she had fallen in love with him in the first place, and why the two of them were meant for each other.

It was not going to be easy with the odds stacked against him, but he was craving the challenge already. His heart jolted whenever he thought of her, even if she didn't believe it. No matter how many reasons she laid down and how many times she stared at him with her spitfire eyes, he would show his wife what happened when he gave a project his undivided attention. Saving this marriage and preserving their love story was indeed a project – a very personal project.

CHAPTER 4

OWEN OPENED THE REAR DOOR TO THE TOWN CAR and Kalilah easily slipped inside.

"My parents' house, please, Owen." She handed him the address.

"Of course, Miss. I take it you had a good meeting then?" her driver prompted.

"It was productive," she returned with a forced smile. She thought back to being so close to Finn and having his body rub against hers. It aroused her immensely and she clenched her thighs at the memory. She told herself that it was a perfectly acceptable reaction to meeting the man she once loved, a man who happened to be her husband even if in name only.

"That's all we can ask for, Miss," He said lightly as he set all his attention to navigating through traffic.

She agreed. She had expected a long, drawn out argument, with Finn pulling rank and throwing the family agreement in her face. However, he never mentioned the agreement. He only talked about the marriage. The last time she was in that office she had caved under her father's threats, because she couldn't imagine a life without the comfort her father's wealth afforded her.

Now life had taught her that money brought a lot of things – things like brand name clothes and servants that took care of her every whim – but it did not buy joy, peace of mind, or time. In fact, it had served as a reminder of what she had lost. Loving a man with all your heart was no guarantee that you wouldn't get hurt. Because it had hurt, badly.

When she had found out the truth behind Finn's interest in her back then, she had felt like running away from the entire situation, but she knew they would find her. Therefore, that idea had quickly flown right out of her mind as quickly as it flew in. Giving in and doing what they wanted had seemed like the path of least resistance. Her father had told her, in no uncertain terms, that if she didn't go through with the marriage that he would cut her off financially, and that she would, in effect, be dead to him. Being young, naïve, and afraid of losing all the comforts she enjoyed, she went through with the wedding. Since her father never specified that she needed to reside with Finn, or even live in the same country as him, she had fled Quebec on the first flight out, before the ink on their marriage paperwork had dried.

***

The first two years away from home had been an uphill climb, and Kalilah had fallen to the bottom several times before she found things she was passionate about. She enjoyed kickboxing and volunteering, passions that she may have never pursued if she'd stayed under her father's watchful eyes. It was through her passion for feeding the homeless that she'd met Jonathan.

On the day she met him, it was frustratingly hot and humid. She'd been trying to haul ten bags of groceries up to her building. The two-bedroom apartment she had leased while in Seattle didn't have a doorman, so she'd struggled to open the building's front door, which was only the beginning of her problems since she lived on the third floor and her building didn't have an elevator. As she was attempting to carry all the heavy bags up to her building, one of them ripped open, spilling some of her groceries onto the sidewalk. She gasped and let out a cuss as she wondered how she was going to retrieve the fallen items without letting go of all the bags she already had.

"They don't make those plastic bags as strong as they used to, but no worries; I got this!"

She turned around, slowly and inquisitively, as she watched a tall, blonde guy crouch over to grab her fallen items. He was handsome, but not as handsome as Finn… but who was comparing? She watched as he gathered them all in his hands, in addition to taking a few bags from her now shaking hands. She'd seen him before. He lived across the street from her apartment, but they'd never shared words before.

"No, they don't," she responded after her arms were free.

"Are you planning on cooking for a small army?" he asked as he felt the weight of the bags in his hands.

She chuckled at his observation and told him about the meals she prepared for the homeless in the community. He seemed impressed with her philanthropy. Carrying her groceries up three flights of stairs, Kalilah stalled once they reached her apartment door. She didn't want to invite a stranger into her home.

"Thanks for all your help. You can place everything down here and I'll carry them inside. I don't know how I would've managed without your help."

"Well, it was no trouble at all helping a beautiful lady such as yourself." He smiled and placed the bags down, and she noticed his teeth were perfect.

"I've seen you around the neighborhood. Are you a student?" He asked.

"Yes," she replied. "My name is Kalilah, by the way".

He reached out his hand and met with hers halfway.

"Jonathan. You can call me Jon though."

"John Doe," she teased, prompting a weird look on his face as he attempted to understand the joke.

He then burst out and started laughing seconds after, prompting a loud laughter from Kalilah as well. After that initial meeting, they would see each other frequently and exchange pleasantries.

Those pleasantries turned into him offering his help whenever she needed something that required muscle. That was the start of a friendship that had blossomed into more, and emotions became more defined. They would go out frequently to movies together, and he would always assist her when she delivered meals to the homeless population.

He had done everything right. Courted her with patience and guidance, while supporting her through troubling times. She'd struggled to understand her own emotions, and what exactly was blooming between them.

Nine months after solidifying their relationship, which they waited a whole year before starting, Kalilah had confessed to him that she was legally married. Surprisingly, he had taken the news rather well, and she was happy he didn't judge her for it. And now she was ready to go all the way with him, but she didn't have it in her to sleep with someone else while she was still legally married, let alone accept a proposal.

She knew she wanted to be with Jonathan, and not even the grueling experience from her first marriage would deter her. She believed in love. Her friends Daria and Ray were happy together. They'd met during the first semester of University, and although Daria was a single mom who had a young daughter, Zoey, with an absentee father, Ray didn't seem to mind one bit. He loved Daria, and since Daria's daughter was a part of her, he had easily fit in with the pair. That was one of the reasons Kalilah didn't return to Canada sooner. She had attended their wedding and the lovebirds couldn't be happier. The last she spoke to Daria, they were in the midst of Ray legally adopting Zoey. Kalilah believed that she deserved a bit of that happiness too.

Her phone rang, knocking her out of her reverie. She dug into her handbag for her phone and finally located it. She smiled as she spied the caller's identity. It brought calmness to her heart, and she answered the phone immediately.

"Hello, angel." The husky baritone washed over her like warm chocolate on a cool day.

"Hi, darling," she replied, and her lips twitched with excitement.

"So, how's dragon hunting going?" He teased. Kalilah smiled at that; those had been her words.

"One down, two to go."

He chuckled at that.

"I have good news and bad news. Good news is that I'll get the annulment with no issues." She was confident about that. "Bad news is I may be here longer than I originally planned."

"How much longer?" All the lightness had dropped from his voice

She told him that it could possibly be over six months. She wanted to have wiggle room in case the paperwork took longer to finalize.

"I can only imagine the legal hassles you're going through," he sighed. "I wish there was something I could do to be of assistance. Maybe I could come up there to offer my emotional support?" His voice filled the car interior.

"I appreciate the offer, darling, but I told you already that this is something I have to do on my own. I got myself entangled in this mess, and it's up to me to get myself out." She sighed; her exhaustion apparent. She loved the fact he offered to help her every chance he got, but she wanted to solve her marriage problems herself. She decided to change the topic, so they spent the remainder of the call discussing trips they would take in the future, as well as a possible date for their wedding.

"Is something the matter, Miss?" Owen asked after she ended the call with Jon.

"No, Owen, everything is just fine," she replied, except it wasn't. She had just lied to her boyfriend. Okay it wasn't a lie, just an omission of what getting the annulment would entail. On top of that, she couldn't seem to shake the yearning that had risen in her at Finn's closeness.

She felt dread rise at the possibilities of what could happen over the next few months.

She wanted to tell Jonathan about the offer Finn had made, but he would not understand.

Convincing him to allow her to come to town alone had caused their first colossal argument.

He'd only backed down when she explained that she needed to do this alone to reclaim her life. She had also promised to keep him in the loop about everything. Even then, it was obvious he didn't understand her desires, but knew he had to let her do things her way. Those moments made her respect him even more.

The car finally slowed down, and Kalilah's attention was drawn to the window. The gates opened and the car went down a long driveway, and past acres of perfectly manicured gardens. Her mother had not lifted one single finger in the creation of this masterpiece. She had only dictated her choices and had her father sign the appropriate cheques. It was magnificent, and she hated it.

The house itself reminded her of her father; large, imposing, and dripping with arrogance. If buildings had attitudes, this one would be smug.

Owen opened the door and Kalilah descended from the car before trekking up the stairs that led to the main door. It swung open on oiled hinges before she got there, and she was met by her first familiar face since her return (Well, she had met Finn, but he didn't count).

"Hello, Bates." Kalilah would have liked to be less formal in addressing him, but her mother frowned on fraternizing with the hired help and that had stuck with her.

"Hello, Miss. Might I take the liberty of saying you look to be in exceedingly good health." The trite words were delivered with twinkling eyes.

"Thank you, Bates, and so do you." She smiled up at her parents' butler. He was an older Caucasian gentleman who towered over her by a couple of feet. His hair was greying at the sides and contained a bald spot in the middle. She used to be friendly with him, sometimes venting her frustrations about her parents to him like he was an uncle or even a friend.

"They are waiting for you in the dining room," he announced.

"So soon." She groaned inwardly. She had been hoping for some time to rest and regroup.

"I think you're not to be given a single respite," he informed her.

"Then it's a good thing I am prepared," she smiled back.

"Very good, Miss," he replied and led her in the direction of the dining room.

"Please, Bates," Kalilah called before he continued on his path. "I can find my way."

"Very well, Miss, and good luck." Kalilah smiled and walked on. She was going to need it. Her session with Finn was intense, but he was nothing compared to the joint force of her parents.

They were the real power behind her marriage five years ago.

***

Kalilah's dad was seated at the head of the table, and her mom was seated on his right. Both of their gazes were stuck on her as she approached the dining room. Kalilah did well to slide into her seat without baring any form of weakness in her demeanor. Kalilah looked from her father to her mother. She had been looking forward to reuniting with her sister, and wondered why Kaiya wasn't at dinner.

"Hello Father. Mother." After they acknowledged her greeting, she asked, "Where is Kaiya?"

They both exchanged looks before her mother replied that she was at a therapist appointment, in a tone that let her know that she wouldn't answer any more questions about Kaiya.

Therapist? She wasn't even surprised that her sister visited a therapist. Growing up in this loveless house could surely push someone to receive therapy.

Supper kicked off without personal enquiries. No words were spoken that were not completely polite, expertly neutral, and full of surface sentiments. They didn't ask about what she had been doing; she was fine. They didn't ask her about work; their family would not tolerate such feminist tendencies. They didn't ask about her five years of self-imposed exile; that was water under the bridge and already long forgotten.

In fact, her moment of rebellion was over, and the consensus was that she had come to her senses to take her place beside her husband, as it should have been all along. The thoughts of their expectations had caused her stomach to tighten in knots. She had mulled over it for hours, before deciding that she couldn't allow them too much power over her life. She had already proven to herself that she could live a happy and full life without them.

Vibrating in anticipation of the battle to come, she surveyed her opponents: Richard Anderson was a man in his prime and, with the aid of good living, that prime was going to last forever. A tall, dark man with touches of silver on his temple gave him a distinguished air. Not that he needed it; he was a clearly a dominant man who ruled his own world. He spooned into his hearty meal with elegant manners that belied his big size. He used to be a God in her eyes, but now, not so much anymore.

Katherine Anderson returned her water goblet to the table with studied grace and signaled the servant to refill her glass. She lifted her glass with her perfectly manicured nails and tilted it at her lips. The motions were languid but assured, backed by the confidence of several years of having her every desire answered. She was beautiful the way a Monet was beautiful.

Mysterious, perfect, evoking strong emotions, but untouchable. One did not hug a Monet; it was a statement of status and class. The perfect accessory. Kalilah had inherited her mother's brown skin and curly hair, but that was where their similarities ended. Her mom seemed to have only two emotions – annoyance and anger. Kalilah had never hugged her mother. Not even when she was a child, or when she had broken her arm after falling from a tree in the backyard. It was her nanny that comforted her, not her mother.

The subdued clink of silver cutlery on fine bone china filled the air, and the soft tread of servants moving in with new dishes and out with the last course was all familiar, but distant.

Kalilah looked down at her untouched meal; the apprehension rolling in her belly had killed her appetite. Besides, she didn't want to be lulled by the false sense of normalcy the room evoked.

Her parents may look benign now, but she knew how fast they would lose those looks if she said or did something that threatened their control or social standing. Divorce being high among those threats.

Her mother signaled and the last course was whisked away. It was time for dessert, and time for the discussion she had been putting off for as long as she could. No more.

"Compliments of the cook, Miss." Kalilah looked down into a generous slice of double chocolate cake. Clear across the room she felt the disapproving stare of her mother. Fraternizing with the hired help was no good for her status. She was barely home and falling from grace already. Not that it mattered; her parents would probably disown her before the night was out.

"Have you seen Finn?" For the first time since the meal began, Katherine Anderson gave her first child her undivided attention.

"I stopped by his office briefly," she returned airily.

"I am sure you two had a lot to talk about," her mother replied.

66

"We did in fact," she muttered as she dug into her desert, the decadent taste filling her mouth.

"When will you be moving in with him?" The question was harmless enough, if one discounted the glint in her mother's eyes. One could see the fete she planned to throw to commemorate the event.

"I thought I could have a few days at home to recuperate," she finally answered as she swallowed down the confection in her mouth.

"From what?" The words were sharp and edged with icicles.

Five years ago, Kalilah would have jumped to remedy her error, now she tossed a bland smile in her mother's direction and cut into her cake.

"Wives belong under the same roof as their husbands." It sounded like a statement but coming from her father it was nothing short of an order. Her mother's discreet nod followed immediately.

Katherine never disagreed or argued with her husband. Was it love, she wondered, or was her mom aware of the hand that fed her, and wrote her cheques? "I still think it was foolish for him to allow you to attend college in another country, but to each man his own. This business of a married woman recuperating anywhere except with her husband is hazy at best and will not be done under my roof," he continued, his booming voice filling the room.

Kalilah became aware that she wouldn't be able to stay here for six months, as she'd hoped. Not when what she wanted was in direct opposition to her parents' desires. She wished Kaiya was here. At least supper would've been more tolerable. She remembered plenty of occasions when Kaiya would secretly text her during supper to mock their parents. Those were good times.

"Go home to your husband, dear; men tend to misbehave when left to their own devices," her mother remonstrated, trying to head off her father's temper.

Is that why you cling to your husband so desperately? The thought, not the words came to Kalilah. Such disrespect would not be tolerated at the table.

"He has been alone for five years."

"More reason to go home to him," her mother insisted.

"Mother, it's hardly been a marriage, and there is no reason to pretend otherwise. Finn would no doubt be more interested in me leaving him to his devices. Apparently, he has done well for himself." She shoved the last fork full of cake into her mouth and cleaned her mouth with the napkin.

"What the boy has done with the company is nothing short of genius; he has the board in his lap. There's no doubt he'll be CEO after I retire." Her dad boasted, like a proud father.

"You're quite right, darling, and Finn has not suffered any lack of social engagements, but you are here now," her mother supplied. The implication was clear.

A wave of jealousy descended on her so sharply her vision wavered. It was too much to believe that a man as handsome or as virile as Finn would play the patient male and wait for his runaway, reluctant bride to return.

Of course he had mistresses stashed in every corner of Quebec, she surmised; more fool she was for allowing herself fall into that five-month game. No biggie. Soon she would return to Jonathan.

Jonathan! Clarity descended with a good dose of shame. Here she was jealous of her husband's social life when she had a boyfriend of her own.

"His social life is his own and will continue to be after I am gone. I did not come home to resume my marriage." It was time to bring her mission to light.

"What are you home for then?"

"I came home to get an annulment." Saying it the second time was easier. Reactions were varied.

Her mother gasped. Her hand flew to her delicate throat and when Kalilah turned to her father, she wished she hadn't.

His brown eyes, much like hers, glittered with barely suppressed anger, and were filled with disbelief. Richard Anderson was not used to having his wishes opposed. He had wanted a competent heir to lead his empire when he no longer could, and had married off his first daughter to get one. Now she was blathering foolishness while seated at his table.

"You cannot do that!" Her mom said. The irony did not escape her; she had said the same thing to Finn earlier today.

"I can, Mother. I met someone new and I want freedom to marry him," she announced calmly.

Her mother was shocked into silence, but not her father.

"Found yourself a smooth-talking gold-digger who's going to take you for all you're worth, girl? I will not allow it!"

"Richard!" her mother gasped again.

"Please, Mother," Kalilah said, and then she turned to her father. "You would know about gold-diggers since you married me to one. Jonathan isn't interested in my money. In fact, he is the best man I've ever met in all my life. Honest to a fault, and kind."

Her father ignored what she had just said and stared at her murderously.

"Finn will never agree to this. That boy loves you too much."

What did her father know about what Finn felt for her anyway? She decided to not offer a response concerning Finn's feelings.

"He already has. In three months' time, I will have my uncontested annulment."

"And you think it's going to be easy? Nothing is final until the judge makes the decision," he pointed out.

"He gave me his word." That stopped the line of questioning. Finn had always proven himself to be a man of his word, a fact that did not escape anyone at that table.

"We cannot change your mind about this?" Her mother asked in a soothing tone. This was the very first time she found her mom's tone to be soothing. She was shocked by it.

"No."

Even if she was deliberately going against them for the first time in her life, there was a little girl inside who still loved her parents. One who wanted their love in return, wanted it so desperately that she was willing to do anything to get it. She needed to smother that inner child.

She looked down to find another slice of chocolate cake on her plate, refusing to pay attention to the heavy air of disappointment that clouded the room; she ate the cake in a haste and then quickly left her parent's home to head to the Ritz. She needed a good night's rest.

***

The darkness was inky black, with tongues of flames chasing away shadows in a dizzying dance. She had only a moment to register before she felt hands skim up her body.

They were hot, and threatened to undo her with their slow pace.

"Please," she moaned into the darkness, begging these hands to stop their slow crawl and end her madness.

There was electricity in her veins and that slow arousal threatened to undo her.

"Please," the hands did not speed up their pace. They took their time to learn the hollows of her body, play on every sensitive spot, skim every stretch of skin except where she needed them to go.

"Please!" Was she begging for this mysterious touch to ravish her, or was she pleading for the delightful torture to stop?

Her lover shifted just enough for the play of light to catch his face. She would recognize that intense blue stare anywhere. The eyes then bled into black and the mop of hair on his head covered his face like a mask.

Kalilah woke up with a gasp.

"No!" One look assured her she was alone, and there was no lover lying in her bed.

She climbed out of bed and ambled into the ensuite bathroom to wash her face. She stood in front of the bathroom mirror and stared at herself for several minutes. The exotic dream now took on the likeness of a nightmare now that she was awake. How could she have dreamt of Finn? One day back, and he'd already wiggled his way into her subconscious.

She had always viewed her dreams as a refuge from reality for many years, and it stung that he had invaded it. And not only did he invade her mind; her body was still humming from the sensory overload the experience had hit her with. She could see the goosebumps on her skin.

Even now, her body strained to finish what had started when she slept.

The phone rang in the other room and she scrambled to catch it before it ended. Saved by the bell.

"Hello?"

The voice that was attached to the face that had invaded her dreams flooded the room.

"Hello Kalilah, how are you?"

"Finn? How did you get my number?"

"I have my ways. I was hoping to finalize a date and time for our first date," he said.

"Ohh," she replied.

"If you're no longer interested..."

She cut in.

"I am always interested in getting my annulment."

"Good. I was hoping you'd want to run away and join the circus with me?"

Kalilah didn't believe her ears. *Circus?* She remembered the first time she told him to take her there. She had the belief that the circus represented freedom and happiness, and that was what she'd felt with Finn years ago. Finn, the smooth talker, had laughed at her suggestion, kissed her affectionately and agreed to move to the circus with her. That promise, he never kept. Now, he had the audacity to bring it up. She fumed at the provocation.

"I know what you're trying to do, and my answer is no." She could see past his patronizing act and she wasn't about to allow him to railroad her into any one of them. He seemed intent on using the past to embroil her.

"Kalilah, you always wanted to run away and join the circus, and that's the point of a date; to do what people enjoy."

"I don't appreciate you using your knowledge of me against me."

He was silent for so long she thought he had dropped the call.

"I understand. How about brunch at the country club?"

"That's fine, when?"

"Tomorrow at eleven am?"

"Sure."

"Are you staying at your parents' estate?"

"Why are you asking?"

He answered and his voice was restrained.

"Just so I know where to pick you up."

How chivalrous, she thought with an eye roll.

"I'll meet you there."

"Look if we're going to do this, it means going the whole nine yards. At least the parts that you're comfortable with for now."

"I'm uncomfortable with you knowing where I'm staying right now," she returned coolly.

"Why? Cause you feel the desire brewing between us? Scared of what you may do?"

"There is nothing brewing between us!" She responded quickly. *Too quickly,* she thought.

Exasperation poured through the phone.

"Keep lying to yourself then. Meet me at eleven am at the country club. Don't be late."

They said their goodbyes and ended the call. Kalilah slumped on the bed with a sigh. Now that she was relaxed, she noticed how tense she had been during the call. He had said there was desire brewing between them. She could lie to him but not to herself. She felt it. He was so far away but he still affected her with just his voice, making a mockery of her declarations in his office earlier today.

Kalilah placed her phone back on the bedside cabinet and snuggled into silk monogrammed sheets. For all the comfort if afforded her, it couldn't remove the ache from between her shoulder blades, a result of having to be strong all day.

She wondered about her younger sister, Kaiya. She hadn't seen nor spoken to her in years, and God did she feel guilty about that. She needed to remedy the estrangement between them as soon as possible.

Kalilah reached for her phone and sighed with disgust at the time. Much too late to call Jonathan; besides she only wanted some comfort to completely erase the effects of her mini-nightmare. She sent him a quick text telling him she loved and missed him.

She still felt guilty, even if she was not at fault. As she rested her head on her pillow, she wondered what could have triggered that kind of dream in her. Her last thought as sleep claimed her, was how wonderful Finn's body felt against hers.

CHAPTER 5

Finn fiddled with the box on the table and looked around the large country club restaurant, trying to catch a glimpse of Kalilah.

Well, he was early. Truth be told, last night he slept fitfully at best. He had given up on trying to sleep as early as five this morning, and had instead gone to the gym for a two-hour intensive workout.

He had shaved, nearly nicking himself in his excitement. He sat down in his bathroom, staring at himself in the mirror, and gave himself a pep talk to tone it down. Then he had gone ahead and driven to her favorite pastry shop to buy her a small, double-chocolate cake. The things love and desperation made a man do.

When he caught sight of her five-foot-seven frame, he had jolted to his feet, scraping the chair back in his enthusiasm. She was dressed in a pink floral dress, which came to just above her knees, and a white jean jacket.

"You're here."

"Was there any doubt?" she replied testily. Yes, there were doubts. Doubts that she would've changed her mind.

"No, please sit." He answered as he pulled out a chair for her, and settled back down in his previously occupied chair.

"So, how does one go about dating their own husband, albeit for only three months?" she started when she had settled into the wicker chair.

"You can begin by telling me about yourself, Madame Anderson," he offered with a wry smile as he took a sip from his coffee.

"You can't be serious. You know who I am."

"I am serious, and besides, we haven't seen each other in years. I want to know more about the woman you are now. Tell me about your life in Seattle and about your school, or even about your hobbies. Je veux tout savoir."

"Really?" Her brow arched. He could tell that he had surprised her.

"Yes, really. Now, tell me about yourself, wife." She gave him a death stare.

Before she could respond to him, the waiter came over to their table and took their orders. After the waiter left to handle their orders Finn continued, "Now, where were we?" He snapped his fingers. "Oh yeah, you were about to tell me all about your life."

And so, the date began. He could tell that she was hesitant at first, but then she finally began to open up a bit. She told him about the small apartment (with no doorman or elevator) she had leased, her school and the few friends she'd made within months of moving to Seattle. She also told him about the degree she completed in Social Work.

"Wow! A degree in Social Work."

"It's been a dream of mine for as long as I could remember."

"I know."

Their food was brought to their table, and the flow of conversation from her end never ceased.

He asked a few questions here and there when he wanted to understand something more clearly. She must have realized that she was doing most of the talking, because she shifted the focus unto him.

"How's work? Father is bursting with pride over what you have done with the company."

"It's a living," he responded easily. "Did you partake in any other activities while in school?"

"I volunteered, mostly at the nearby homeless shelter for women, whenever I had a break from school." She smiled, and he saw the happiness in her eyes. "I've met many amazing people through my humanitarian work, and I have many fond memories. I also have memories I wish I could forget. You wouldn't believe it if I told you that a high percentage of the population are just a paycheck away from being homeless. We have so much, and there are people out there with nothing."

"Wow, Lilah, you've done so much for the world." He was very proud of her. "What do you intend to do with your degree now that you're a graduate?" He could tell the question had both shocked and pleased her.

"I've been thinking of opening my own shelter for homeless women and young mothers, but for now I'll stick to volunteering at different shelters. I want to gain more experience and find out what's lacking in the services being provided. I have no need to have a paying job, as it may be taking a job and salary away from someone else that needs it more than me. I just want to make a difference, no matter how small."

"That's very thoughtful and admirable of you. I've never thought about it that way. I'm proud of the woman you've become, Lilah. You did it on your own, and I couldn't be prouder of you. I think you should go ahead and open the shelter, and I'll help you in whatever way I can." He truly meant it. He recently acquired an apartment complex that needed some TLC, and he would happily give it to her if she was truly serious about helping people who were less fortunate than them. He loved her, and if having her own organization where she made a difference would make her happy, then he'd see that she got it.

"Thank you. So, any altruistic reasons for being in real estate?"

"Just playing the demand and supply game," he answered.

"And playing it well I see. I believe it has to be more than that." As a kid he had watched HGTV. Unlike other kids, who watched cartoons, he'd preferred to watch TV shows where people got matched to their dream homes.

When he still didn't answer, she prompted, "So?"

"It's the thrill of matching the perfect land to the perfect use. It's like filling the perfect puzzle. It doesn't hurt when I make a load of cash from that too. Satisfied customers are a beautiful thing."

"I'll bet," she replied. And another silence descended on the table.

***

She felt eyes on her, and when she lifted her gaze, she found Finn was staring at her intently.

81

"What are you looking at?"

"I see you still indulge yourself with food."

She raised her brow.

"So?"

"I just think its super sexy how you're not afraid to eat."

"Is that your way of saying I've put on weight?"

"No, not at all. And to show you I meant no harm, take this." He proffered the small box he had been fiddling with, and Kalilah took the proffered box with confusion. It was too small to contain the annulment papers she so desperately wanted.

"Go ahead, it won't bite, I promise," he promised softly.

She loosened the strings that were wrapped around the box. The smell hit her first and had her salivating before she saw the entirety of the package.

Damn, this is what she got for fraternizing with the enemy. No soul alive could resist a double chocolate cake from Angel Fair.

"I see that you still have a weakness for chocolate cake." Finn gloated, but Kalilah was too busy transferring the delectable morsel onto her plate to pay him any mind.

One forkful and she was in nirvana. She barely held in the moan, but she didn't care.

He took a sip of his steaming coffee and leaned toward her, his strong body filling her vision. His citrus scent hit her at close quarters, and her nose flared to take in the scent. Mixed with the aroma of chocolate, it was intoxicating.

"Are you enjoying the taste of it? Still good as you remember?"

"Hmmmm," Kalilah nodded her head slowly in affirmation, all the while munching on it with her eyes closed.

"So good," she breathed, and the single word jolted her back to the incident she was determined to chalk up as a mini-nightmare.

He gestured playfully at her plate with a fork, and laughed when Kalilah quickly pulled the plate away from his reach. She looked at him to see upturned lips and a twinkle in his eye, and tried to refocus her attention to her cake but she couldn't help but to look up at Finn again. They both chuckled at her actions, their gazes locked together.

She dropped the fork to the plate with a light clatter as she reached for her cup of orange juice. Finn reached across the table, and his sudden movement jarred her backward, breaking the spell that melded their eyes.

"You just have a spot of chocolate on you," he explained.

"Where?"

He told her where it was, and she dabbed the spot.

"Look, Lilah, I want us to have a future together." She opened her mouth to shut him down, but he cut off what she was about to say with a hand gesture. "Before you came back to Montréal, I'd already made up my mind to come find you in Seattle and bring you home. My jet was set to leave for the US next week." He reached into the back of his pants pocket and produced the flight itinerary; it was a one-way trip with no return date.

She was shocked. She didn't know what to think or how to respond to what he'd just said. He spoke again before she could put together a response for him.

"I am prepared to do anything so that we can get back everything that we lost. I'm not giving up on us."

She was taken aback by how determined he sounded. Before she could think more about what he said he continued.

"I don't think Jamie is the right man for you."

"His name is Jonathan, and you don't? I wonder why?" she started sarcastically. "You and my father seem preoccupied with telling me what you think is best for me. Are you the right man for me? Considering what happened years ago and how much money was involved or implied." It was the perfect blow to land; she could see that he lost some of his cockiness by the way his eye twitched.

"I didn't take a dime from your father. I had honorable intentions, Lilah!" Finn answered, and she registered the fury in his voice.

"No, but you took his cash cow," she retorted.

"I married the woman I fell in love with. Your dad gave his blessings for the marriage along, with an offer for a position in his company. Nepotism is hardly uncommon."

"You started this mess, Finn, by agreeing to marry me in exchange for the company. All I did was get away to protect myself," she informed him coolly.

"Without listening to my version of events," he added coolly, before raising a hand to summon the waiter, effectively cutting off any reply. He was right; she'd never given him the opportunity to explain his side of things, and she was wondering now if that was a mistake. She'd been so sure that he'd used her to get ahead in the company that she'd ignored his many attempts at making things right. Her mind drifted back to the past, when she confronted Finn after overhearing his conversation with her father.

He walked up to her and took her in his arms.

"Babe, please listen, you misunderstood what your father said. We…"

"Did my father not agree to give you a position within the company if you got married to me?"

She was heated, embarrassed.

"No, Lilah, listen, I…"

She cut him off again.

"You're still lying to me, Finn. I heard the conversation between the two of you. I can't believe you used me that way.

I loved you, and you used me. You used the love I had for you to further your own interest with my father." She was sobbing now.

"Babe, please, just listen to me. I love you. There is no one else for me." Tears were streaming down his face, but his steady speech never deviated. "I would never hurt you, Lilah. Please. Believe me – I would never hurt you. I want to marry you, only you."

"So why did you make this deal with my father then?" She stepped out of his embrace. She didn't want to be so close to him. His arms no longer brought the comfort they once did.

"Because I love you."

She couldn't believe the shit he was saying. How did using her as a bargaining chip for a company equate to love?

She'd turned her back on him and gone home. That night she told her father that she would not marry Finn, and that their engagement was off. He merely asked her if Finn abused her physically, and she had vehemently protested that question. Even though he had hurt her, she still felt protective of him. She explained to him that she wouldn't be a pawn in his business plans. Her father laughed at her explanation for breaking up the engagement and told her that she would marry Finn whether she wanted to or not. When she still refused, he threatened to cut her off financially if she didn't do as he asked. She had felt so alone in that moment. The first thing on her mind was to run away, but she knew they'd find her. So, in the end, she'd decided to go through with the wedding – which took place a week later – and then she'd left Canada an hour later. She'd taken a taxi to Pierre Trudeau Airport, and got the first flight out. Finn had come a week later to bring her home and she had refused to even talk to him.

Did she throw her entire marriage away over a simple misunderstanding? That realization halted her breath. She couldn't have any regrets now. It was too late to think of what she could have done differently.

Her mind was brought back to the present when she heard a chair being moved. Finn got up, walked over to her, and eased back her chair. He must have paid for their meal while she was thinking of the past. She didn't want to be rude since he paid for breakfast, so she offered him a soft smile as she thanked him. Finn walked Kalilah toward the awning where Owen was parked out front, waiting for her. He gave Owen a curt nod and turned to her.

"Should I broach the topic of our next date?"

"No circuses. In fact, let's not bring up anything from the past."

His eyes widened but he nodded at her two conditions.

"I was hoping for lunch?"

"I can do lunch."

"Tomorrow?"

"I'll let you know; I'll have to check to see if I'll be available," she replied curtly. She needed time to regroup and think about everything that she'd learned today. She also didn't want him to think that she was always available for his whims. She wanted to take things slow.

"I see… amazing how quickly one's social calendar can fill after being away from home for so long." His eyes locked onto hers and she took small consolation in her ability to hold his gaze without losing her confidence. "Do call me when you have your affairs settled. I'll expect to hear from you by this evening."

He walked away and headed off in the direction of the golf course. She looked over Finn's receding back and thought about how sexy he looked walking away, just as much as when he had been walking toward her earlier. Broad shoulders, narrow waist, toned legs. She closed her mind to her current thoughts and turned towards the car. Before she could reach for the handle, Owen outdid her and helped her in.

"May I?" he said, taking a mock bow and doffing an imaginary hat.

***

During the date with Kalilah, Finn came to the same conclusion he had reached in his office. He still loved her and was extremely happy about her growth. She was living her dreams, and it was clear that there was no place for him in her life. He would have to fight for her, and for a place in her life. He remembered the glow in her eyes as she spoke about everything she accomplished while she was away, and felt a little envious. Her eyes used to glow that way before, when she spoke of him; now her eyes only bore resentment in his direction.

"Is everything alright?" Gabe asked him. Gabe and Finn met at the golf course, where Finn accused him of not using his height well. His exact wording was "you should be playing basketball and not golf. Trust me; if I had that height of yours, I would be an NBA champion now," Finn said. Gabe found him funny and they got to talking and became friends.

He hit the golf ball with a club, and it landed in a hole.

"I'm good," Finn said, immediately regretting not making it convincing.

"Listen, we've played many times before, and every time I see you, you ask about Steph and pick my brain about the financial feasibility of that mall you're wanting to build, but not once today have you asked about either. Talk to me, tell me what's bothering you."

Finn held the tip of his golf club and took deep breathes.

"Am I that easy to ready?"

"Not usually."

Finn sighed.

"I don't even know where to start."

"From the beginning. What is eating you up, dude?'

"My wife..."

"Wife?" He could see the shock on the other man's face. Finn had never told him about his marital woes.

"Yes, my wife. I'm a married man." Finn took the next 20 minutes to tell his friend all about him and Kalilah. He didn't leave any details out. By the time he was done he could see that his friend was stunned. "...and now she is back seeking an annulment."

Gabe burst into laughter; tears were streaming down his face. He pulled out a brown handkerchief and wiped his face, and Finn was trying to figure out what part of his misery was funny.

"Is my life a huge joke to you?" Finn was beginning to get annoyed.

"No," Gabe said, still trying to contain his laughter, it came anyway. "It... it is just so funny. Your wife abandons you for five years, meets a new man, comes back to town and the first thing she asks for is an annulment?"

Finn gave no response. He knew how messed up the situation was without having someone narrate it to him.

"Wow! That is some deep shit. I am so sorry for you. I can only imagine how she must feel..."

"You are supposed to be on my side here," Finn said.

"I am on your side. I can only imagine how you must feel too, especially with regard what you told me. Have you told her your part of the story?"

Finn picked up a golf ball.

"I have tried to talk to her, but you know how it is. She doesn't want to listen; she still feels I am a user," Finn said as Gabe listened keenly. Finn hit the golf ball, and it landed in a hole. "We had a date…"

"You had a date?" Gabe asked

"Yes, I'm trying to win her over."

"I am lost, dude."

"I refused to give her the annulment, and I told her that I would do that on one condition."

"What is the condition?"

He told Justin his conditions and he could see amusement and shock on his friend's face.

"And she agreed?"

"Yes, very quickly too. She's determined to get these dates over with so she could resume the life she started in the States," Finn added bitterly.

Gabe looked at his friend and shook his head in pity.

"All I see is a woman who is determined to move on. She left everything, her father's money and her husband, to start life again without any support. Now, she is here, she has fallen in love with someone else, and the only reason she is here is to get her marriage annulled. I am sorry, dude."

"I hope you are going somewhere with this."

"Give her the annulment and move on."

"Not happening."

"By giving her what she wants, you'll be free to meet other women and move on yourself."

"What Kalilah and I once shared can't be explained, it was unique; it was pure, it was deep, it was true love. I know for a fact that what she has with this new man doesn't hold a candle to what we had together. I could feel the chemistry between us and even though her mind and lips will deny it, I know her body and heart won't. A love like that doesn't just go away, Gabe. Kalilah and I belong together, and I am going to work hard to make sure I win her back. She is my future."

"Damn, dude, I hope it works out for you, but I don't know." Gabe said, hitting the golf ball into a hole. The two men spent the remainder of the afternoon playing golf and discussing business. Finn heard everything Gabe said, but he chose not to dwell on it. His intentions remained solely on winning his wife over.

CHAPTER 6

ON THE RIDE TO HER PARENTS' HOUSE, she thought back to everything that transpired during brunch. She didn't expect for their first date to go so well. She would be lying if she didn't admit that she was happy she had impressed Finn. When she'd asked him about work, Kalilah had expected him to pick up the ball and go with it. She expected him to extol himself for the next thirty minutes or so about how awesome he was at his job. Finn had merely smiled, and she fancied she caught sincerity in his smile.

When she'd met with her parents yesterday evening, there was no question of work; in fact, it was already decided that she was going to be the perfect trophy wife, who could hold conversations on diverse topics. However, Finn praised her for finding her passions in life. She was genuinely surprised by his demeanor, although she didn't understand why. This man was the man she fell for years ago. He hadn't changed, she surmised. She had; she was more cynical. And that realization threatened to send her into a tailspin.

The sincerity in his words touched her heart, and she soaked it all up like she had been waiting forever to hear them. The biggest shocker came when he showed proof that he was going to come back for her. And she wondered what she would have done if he showed up to her apartment. She would've been so unprepared, which would have given him the upper hand.

She was the one who had left him. Left their marriage. He'd always been here waiting. Waiting on her. In her heart of hearts, she knew that simple truth, but she couldn't get past his betrayal.

She'd loved him so much, and he'd hurt her so terribly. But the pain from that betrayal didn't sting as much as it had when she'd first learned of it. She wondered, again, what that meant for her future.

***

There were a few things Kalilah was sorry for. Three things, maybe four.

One, she had allowed herself to love the wrong man and, in the end, had cultivated pain from falling hard for him. The

94

second was allowing her parents to railroad her and thus steal precious moments of her life. The third was waiting to take back her life. She always advised her women in the shelter to seize control of their life, and to not allow selfish people to steal away their joy. Some tried, but it wasn't easy. She had not been able to fully embrace the desire to do so until Jonathan came along and questioned why she kept her life on hold.

At the time she didn't think her life was on hold, since she was living her dreams away from her family. When he had finally questioned her about the two of them building a future and starting a family, she began to question herself about why she was still legally tied up with Finn. She supposed that in the depths of her heart, where that naïve girl still resided, she had always held out a sliver of hope for her and Finn. And that legal connection made it so that they would always have a connection. She couldn't hold out on living her life any longer. Taking control became paramount.

The fourth regret was her sister. Probably her biggest regret. The past five years had been so tumultuous that Kalilah's relationship with her sister had been affected too. Of course, they still spoke, but it was never meaningful. The extent of their conversations never went past *'Hey, what's up? Nothing, you? Nothing.'*

She was embarrassed to say the least, and being the older sister by five years didn't help soothe the guilt for not making more of an effort. She should have made more of an effort, considering how cold their parents were. She had convinced herself that her sister's strong-willed personality would see her through, and that their sibling bond would be okay. She had issued several invitations to her sister to come up to Seattle and have a fun-filled girls' weekend, but it never happened. Her sister had spent a whole year in New Brunswick when she was seventeen, and she never found out why. It was her mother who had informed her, while she was at college, about Kaiya's move to a new province. However, when her sister did return to Quebec, both her parents and her sister never bothered to give her any explanations as to why she'd moved away. The last time they had spoken, Kaiya didn't divulge any information about herself, so she figured it was her own way of telling her not to delve into her affairs.

They were like two sides of the same coin. Her sister was the cheerful one, with a charming personality and liked by everyone. Kalilah was the opposite, she was the more studious one who never broke the rules. However, they were both passionate about their interests in life.

Kaiya had always loved dance, and Kalilah had always been drawn toward helping people who got referred to as NH. Nonhuman. Kaiya had always done ballet, and had joined the cheerleading squad at their private secondary school. She was exceptional at both.

Lilah on the other hand, was the brainiac who always scored high in academics and lived to please her parents. Lilah had thought of Finn as her salvation. How foolish she had been.

Growing up, Kaiya had gotten less attention from their parents, and it made her a bit wild. Kaiya played pranks on the staff and snuck out at fifteen, with Kalilah's ID with her best friend Jalissa, who Kaiya had met in seventh grade. Kaiya never really got reprimanded. With Kalilah however, everything was monitored and controlled. Because of their age difference, they grew distant when Kalilah became a teenager. She knew her sister had changed after returning to Quebec from her mysterious New Brunswick move. She became more withdrawn and focused on her dancing.

She had given her sister space, and figured that she would find out what was going on when she returned to Montréal. But then she became busy with her school, the shelter, and working on her thesis. Self-condemnation threatened to be her undoing as she felt tension building in her muscles. They hadn't spoken with each other in over a year, and that was a long time.

Guilt may have propelled her to tell Owen to drive her to her parents' house, but sisterly love had her lifting her head to smile as Kaiya walked out the front door, before she had the chance to step out of the car.

"Hey, gorgeous," Kalilah said in a cheery tone. Kaiya's head snapped up when she heard the voice and looked around until she found the caller.

"Oh-em-gee! You're back!" Her sister squealed. Kalilah got out of the car and the sisters ran toward each other. They collided in a full-body hug mid-run.

"Hey silly bird, want to hang out with me today?" Kalilah asked her sister, hoping from the smile on Kaiya's face and the excitement in her voice that she'd come with her. When she'd left, her sister was shorter than her, now she towered over her by a few inches.

"Hello, yellow." The belated nickname from childhood seemed very inappropriate right now.

From up close, her chestnut skin glowed. Despite the beauty of her skin, her once-lively light brown eyes seemed hollow. Kaiya's hands tightened with a kind of desperation around her. It was as if Kaiya was afraid that if she let go of her sister, she would miraculously disappear. The way she had done for five years. That damn guilt... Kalilah winced. This wasn't the same playful sister of hers who always bustled with life. *What broke her spirit?* Kalilah thought, perplexed.

"Sorry." Her sister jerked away from the embrace. "I am so sorry." The apologies were unnecessary. Kalilah wondered why, exactly, her sister was apologizing, and what for. Wrinkles formed on her brow as she looked Kaiya over, trying to find an explanation.

Kalilah couldn't bear it.

"There's nothing to apologize for, I promise." Kaiya's countenance reminded her of every mirror she'd looked into after leaving Finn. In fact, it was eerily similar to the way new arrivals to the shelter looked.

Kalilah's hand tightened around her sister's wrist and pulled her toward the car.

"You're coming to lunch with me." It wasn't an invitation, it was more of a statement, an order, and her sister submitted meekly, rousing a fresh wave of guilt. She knew better than that, or at least she should. "You don't have any plans, do you?"

Kaiya took one look at the mansion and back at her sister's car with the low purr of the engine. Her answer came so quietly that even Kalilah almost missed it.

"Are you kidding me, of course I want to have lunch. Let's get out of here!" It was more than an acceptance of a lunch invitation, and not for the first time Kalilah wondered what had happened in her absence.

If any child had to wonder if she really belonged to her parents, then it was Kaiya. Not only was her temperament soft, bubbly, and sweet, but Kaiya couldn't hold a grudge and she often cried in moments of intense anger.

There was no hint of the soft, sweet, bubbly girl today, though.

Something seemed to have stripped her of everything, until she was all skin, bones, and eyes.

Kalilah had an inclination of who was responsible for that: their parents. Her hand tightened on her sister's, and Kaiya squeezed her back. Some things were bigger than her impending divorce; she wouldn't sit back and watch them suck the soul out of her sister the way they had tried to do to her all those years ago.

She held Kaiya's hand with a determined will to protect her. After all, that's what older sisters did, protect their siblings. And she would do just that. She needed to make up for her absence.

Hand in hand, they strutted to the car to meet the waiting Owen.

Owen drove without a firm destination for a while, before he turned off Atwater Avenue onto the smaller road of Saint Emelie Street. Kalilah took one look at the Atwater Market, and it brought back many fond memories of spending her Saturday mornings here during summer, inhaling the sweet scent of garden-fresh fruits and delicious food. She immediately scrapped any idea of lunch at some sophisticated location, or even back at her hotel restaurant.

"Owen, stop the car." And the black marvel of engineering quietly edged to the curb. "You don't mind if we walk do you? Kalilah asked. "The day is much too beautiful to be spent indoors."

Truthfully, it was one of those perfect summer days; the humidity wasn't too bad, and not a single cloud lingered overhead. Kaiya nodded and opened her door, with her sister climbing out at the same time, unwilling to let go of her hand.

"Where should I wait for you, Miss?" Owen asked.

"Find a suitable parking spot, Owen, and maybe grab something to eat. I don't know how long we'll be, or where we are going to end up, but I will give you a call the moment we are done and ready to return," she directed.

"Of course, Madame." They got out of the car and he drove off, leaving them in the midst of the large crowd. Something had broken Kaiya's lethargy, and she literally threw herself into the day with a vigor that Kalilah thought bordered on manic. Thank goodness! It was one other thing she was grateful for in her choice of college course. Studying social work granted her the opportunity of taking courses in psychology and, leaning on that knowledge, Kalilah was certain there was something maladaptive about Kaiya's behavior. She just couldn't place it yet.

They moved from shop to shop without a word. Occasionally her sister would fondle a child's toy or a piece of baby clothing.

"Is there something I should know? Am I going to be an aunt?" Kalilah asked apprehensively.

"If you're ever going to be an aunt, it won't be from me," Kaiya responded, and quickly walked off in another direction. Kalilah didn't know what to make of what her sister said, so she continued her perusal of the merchandise. The better part of an hour was spent window shopping, until they stood in front of a shop that offered the freshest produce and cups of coffee.

Kalilah inclined her head, and Kaiya followed almost meekly. They had barely settled in when the waiter was at their table. His bright smile was wasted on the two of them; they were offered a plate of the special with cups of juice and coffee.

When the food came, Kaiya moved her fork around the untouched pasta while staring into the distance. Kalilah took her time to observe her sister; exile be damned, she had failed her favorite person and best friend.

"You've changed a lot; I kind of have to look at you sideways to recognize you." Her sister was thinner than she remembered, if that was possible. Kalilah guessed that her sister was about 110lbs, and considering she was about five-foot-seven, she was petite. Her long hair that she had always kept in a huge, messy 'fro – which always infuriated their mother, who had always criticized her about the mass of unruly curls hanging loose – was now slicked back in a bun. She also had dark circles under her eyes, and her smile that used to come to her face so easily was nowhere to be found.

"Change is inevitable. I had no choice but to grow up," Kaiya answered after a moment of silence. Kalilah sensed from the tone of her voice that her sister was on the verge of tears.

"I understand. I guess I can say the same thing myself. Did you come back to stay?"

Kalilah shook her head and tried to suppress the surge of guilt that threatened to drown her this time. Her plans had no place for her sister.

"I only came back to get an annulment from Finn. And them," she added as an afterthought.

"Our parents aren't so bad; they've helped me a lot." And for the first time since they started talking, Kaiya stared at her sister. Her skin had lost its earlier glow, and her eyes were shuttered and resigned. All this combined had her suddenly terrified to know what happened to her sister.

"How did they help you?" Kalilah ventured tentatively. She didn't believe for a second her parents would help anyone but themselves.

"They were there for me, okay. And you weren't," Kaiya responded, but it didn't sound accusing – more matter-of-fact.

Kalilah swallowed hard, her guilt rising again.

"It's okay if you don't want to talk about it. I understand." Seriously, it stung. She never thought she would be using her own skills on her sister. Eyes level, voice neutral but projected with confidence, and some empathy to invite trust.

"I do want to tell you about everything that happened, but not yet, maybe later. Just not right now."

"Okay. I'll accept that... so, what do you want to do now?"

"Let's just sit here for a while before we go shopping again, I will try to finish my food." Lilah tactfully didn't want to point out that they didn't buy anything the first time around. Thankfully Kaiya averted her attention to her meal in such a leisurely way that even Lilah noticed that every spoon was a personal debate. Every gulp, every swallow was a single choice.

"So, what are you up to these days anyway? Still hoping to join a professional ballet group?" Kalilah suddenly spoke catching Kaiya off guard. Lilah remembered how determined her younger sister was to join Les Grandes Ballets Canadiens de Montréal.

"I... I no longer have any interest in joining a ballet company," Kaiya stammered.

Kalilah was shocked by that admission. She wondered if their parents knew. *Well, of course they knew,* she surmised. She placed her hands on Kaiya's and spoke softly.

"Are you serious? You can't be serious. How come?" she asked, all without taking a breath.

"So much has happened, and I guess I no longer feel the appeal I once felt for professional ballet." Her face lit up as she continued. "I have decided instead to open my own dance school for young girls."

"Really? That's a grand endeavor. I'm proud of you." Kalilah said encouragingly.

"Yes, I know, right? I'm nervous, but excited!" She all but squealed. A shadow then came over her face and she cast her eyes down. "Don't be mad when I say this, but Finn has been helping me find a place that will be big enough for the school."

Kalilah's eyes grew wide at that admission. This was the last thing she was expecting to hear from her Kaiya. She didn't think Finn would care what her sister had going on. A lot had changed since she left, she supposed, even her husband. *Soon to be ex-husband,* she reminded herself. She didn't want to concern herself with what he was up to, but she couldn't help but wonder. She squeezed her sister's hand.

"That's nice of him, I suppose." She responded. She couldn't say more, and didn't want to either.

"Yes, it is, we have more buildings to visit, but my heart is almost set on one building we saw last week in the West Island, on Pierrefonds Boulevard."

"I am so proud of you, sis. Tell me more about your school."

Feeling a bit put off by everything she'd just learned, she went back to her meal and left Kaiya to do most of the talking – about her plans for the school – for the rest of their meal. Listening to her sister happily discuss her plans about the school made her happy. It gave her hope for her own future.

They spent the second half of the day in a more jovial mood than the first. They went shopping; Kaiya finally bought a soft cashmere shawl, a silver wind chime small enough to hand over a baby's crib, and soft silver bangles that matched them in tone. They spoke in depth about things that had happened since they were last together. Kaiya never ventured into whatever it was their parents had helped her with, but her Kalilah didn't mind. She told Kaiya about Seattle and Jonathan. She also told her about the times she volunteered in the shelters, and the wonderful women she had met. When they were finished shopping and catching up, Kalilah hugged her sister and then texted Owen to pick them up.

After getting seated in the back of the car, she brought up the idea that had been running around in her mind throughout their outing.

"Do you want to stay with me? I know I'll be gone soon, but I'm going to be here for a little while and I want to spend time with my favorite sister. I'll have to get a condo obviously, because I can't stay at the Ritz forever, so are you in?"

Kaiya's brows knitted together, as if in deep thought, until she answered with a short nod and hid her tears against her sister's shoulder. Kalilah looked away only to catch Owen's eye in the rearview mirror. He nodded at her too.

"I'm so glad you're back, Lah," Kaiya sniffled, "Even though it's only for a little while. I missed you."

***

Finn's mom Lawrence's face lit up with joy as he stepped through the living room. She came to him immediately and offered him a big hug. He had driven two hours from Montréal to Ottawa to see his family. The last time he saw his mom was last Christmas. At the time she was complaining about losing weight and had decided to jump on the keto train. It looked as if the keto life had been working for her.

She was trim and slim, better than the last time Finn saw her. Lawrence ran a keto blog and had even started a YouTube channel. He was glad to be around his family, even though it wouldn't be a long visit. His 22-year-old siblings came over and gave him a hug. Julia was as gorgeous as their mom, and Justin was as tall as Finn but not as broad in the shoulders; he looked more like their dad, especially with his grey eyes. Finn and Julia inherited their mom's blue eyes. Finn's dad, Alexandre, came up to him, and intense grey eyes gave him a once over before he pulled him into a hug.

"I missed you, son!" said Alexandre. His mom had met and married the man when Finn was five years old. After they got married, Alexandre had adopted Finn, and never saw him as anything less than his son. Finn was happy for the man's presence in his life. Finn had never met his biological father and knew very little about the man except that he was Irish. "How long are you staying?" He asked as he pulled away from the hug.

"A few hours. I need to get back." Finn missed the knowing look that passed between his mom and dad.

"How do you like the fat bomb?" Lawrence asked Finn, almost an hour after his arrival, and he made a face. 'Come on; it is tasty. It is dark chocolate and pecan, the keto way. Can't you see how healthy I am looking? It will do you a lot of good, young man, to eat healthily, so you do not look like a bag of potatoes when you are older,' she said sternly. The family burst into laughter. Julia almost choked on her snack.

"Since mom started this and her channel blew, it has been from one keto thing to another, she is always creating different recipes," Julia whispered into Finn's ear, and he snorted.

"What are you to whispering about?"

"Nothing that would interest you," Finn responded.

"Don't think because you are modeling for magazines..."

"I am not modeling for magazines, mom, the magazines are doing a profile on young businessmen," he said.

"I am glad you are living your dreams," Lawrence said.

"I am not living my dreams," Finn protested. His dreams included his wife, and since she was hell bent on being away from him, his dreams still hadn't been actualized. He bit into the fat bomb with more force than necessary and was very surprised – it was delicious. He didn't let his mom know that, either.

"Flying from province to province, and even internationally, in addition to having beautiful women throw themselves at you, seems like a dream to me. Miss me with the fake humility, bro. We love you, humble or proud," said Justin.

"I still think you would be an asset to my chain of franchises, Finn. Leave real estate and let us put your business degree into better use," he said. Everyone was silent, including his mom.

They'd had this same conversation many times before, and his response was always the same.

"I love what I do..."

"You love business, not real estate; you know how to create profit and seal deals. That is why I want you on my team. Think of everything we can achieve together as a family. We sent you to school to get a degree and use the degree to grow our business. We are glad that you have gained business experience working with Richard, but don't you think it is time you come home?"

"Dad, Montréal is my home. Always has been." Now that Kalilah was back, it would probably be his home for a while longer. His home would be wherever she was.

"Homes change."

"Kalilah came back to Montréal..."

After several minutes of silence his mom finally said, "Really?" He looked at the rest of his family and no one seemed surprised by his admission.

"You all knew?" he asked.

"I saw Kaiya's post on Instagram and I showed it to mum." Julia told him.

"I didn't know you kept in touch." Finn said, seriously surprised.

"We don't keep in touch, but we're kind of family, so we follow each other on social media sites."

"So, are you two finally going to work out your problems and resume your marriage?" asked his dad. Of course he'd assume that.

Finn cleared his throat and adjusted his position; he sat back in his chair.

"She wants to put an end to the marriage."

"That's understandable," Justin said.

"Hush, Justin," said Julia. "Finn still loves her, don't you Finn?"

Lawrence gave a threatening stare to her younger children and then turned compassionate eyes unto her eldest son.

"How are you feeling about this?"

"I have no intentions of ending this marriage. I have waited for her for five years, and she strolls back into town and thinks that I'll let all these years spent apart go down the drain over a stupid misunderstanding. Never. I know she still loves me, and even if she doesn't, I have to try mom. She needs to know that I never used her."

"You're still young, son, and have time to meet someone else and start anew. As much as I like the girl, I can't forget that she left you without even a backward glance. I say divorce her and move on," said Alexandre. Justin nodded his agreement, and Julia looked ready to oppose their dad.

Lawrence stood up and yelled, "Out! All of you out! I want to talk to my son without interference!"

Everyone knew when not to oppose her, so they all quickly filed out of the dining room.

"Now that we're alone, we can talk." She gave him a small smile. "I understand what you're saying, Finn, but do you think it's for the best? Not only for her, but for you as well."

He considered what his mom asked him, and knew that being with the woman he loved above all else was for the best. He wouldn't give up on them now. He had paid enough for a crime he never committed. It was time to collect on the grievance.

"Mom, I know what I am doing, and I know what's at stake here." His mom didn't seem convinced, and he didn't have the energy to convince her. There was only one woman he needed to convince, and she was back in Montréal.

"I had always hoped that you and Kalilah would work things out, but now I'm not so sure. You've been away from each other for so long. So many things could have happened in that time..." His mom didn't know the half of it. Kalilah had a boyfriend now, but he wouldn't tell his family about that. He didn't want his family to view her negatively, especially since he was trying to work on their marriage.

"Mom, it's okay." He stood up and went over to her and gave her a hug. "Kalilah and I will be fine; you'll see."

"Promise me one thing."

"Anything except giving up on my marriage."

She smiled at him.

"I know your mind is made up about winning your wife over, so I won't waste my breath to dissuade you. I want you to be happy, Finn, and I know that Kalilah did make you happy, but I also know how crushed you were after she left. Remember, you can't force these things, these matters of the heart. I would know. I was depressed after your dad walked away from us, from you. Promise me that you'll prepare yourself in case things don't go your way, and that you'll move on. It is for your own good, son; I do not want you to die of heartbreak."

Finn smiled.

"I promise, Mom. I even promise to move here to Ottawa if things don't go as planned." He knew he would never move to Ottawa.

CHAPTER 7

TWO DAYS LATER, AFTER TRAIPSING AROUND OLD
PORT all day with her sister, they walked through the door of
Kalilah's hotel suite, giggling like schoolgirls at a meme they'd
just seen on social media. She hadn't heard from Finn in the
past few days and, honestly, she was a bit relieved. She had
enjoyed the time she and her sister were spending together.
She sent Jonathan a quick text to let him know she had
arrived back in her room. She hadn't spoken to Finn since
their brunch date, and she was okay with that. They had
barely settled into the room when her phone rang. Kalilah
looked at the screen thinking it was her beau, but her
shoulders tensed when she saw who was calling.

"Hello, Finn," she answered coolly.

"Kalilah, how are you doing on this fine summer evening?" He started.

"I was doing much better before I got this call."

He ignored her statement.

"What do you think about supper?"

"It's an important meal of the day, it really shouldn't be skipped," she evaded, unwilling to make things easier for him. She wanted to spend the evening with her sister, and she would.

"And having it with me?" He was not deterred by her evasion.

"It's impossible tonight."

"You're not being difficult just to avoid being around me, are you? Are you afraid of what may happen between us if you spend time with me?" he challenged.

Of all the arrogant annoying things to say, it made her even more determined to keep him at arm's length.

"Avoiding you will not get me what I want, now will it?"

Finn cleared his throat over the phone and huffed. He only did that when he was completely irritated and desperately trying to keep his cool. It gave Kalilah a perverse thrill that she was the cause of his annoyance. She knew it was petty, but she was willing to take all she could get.

She remembered him making that same sound years ago, when he'd picked her up from her friend Kayla's family barbecue. Kayla's brother was flirting with her at the time, and she didn't do much to rebuff his advances since she knew he was a harmless flirt and did that with most girls.

Finn had been angered, and almost came to blows with the younger man. She had kissed him into oblivion that day to calm him, and promised him that she only had eyes for him. She had been so happy then.

She buried the memory quickly in that emotional grave where she kept all other memories from that time. She just wished they could stay buried and not reappear to haunt her thoughts like ghosts.

"I just want to have supper with you, preferably tonight."

"I can't. Look, things are a bit hectic," she said, hoping to dissuade him.

"Is your boyfriend visiting?" He asked in a growl and she wondered why he would assume her boyfriend's visit to be the reason for her not being free.

Kalilah swallowed her indignation and gritted her teeth.

"No, not that it's any of your business but I just want to spend time with my sister."

That stopped him short.

"Oh, how is Kaiya doing, anyway? We have a meeting soon."

She remembered suddenly that Kaiya and Finn were dance school hunting.

"She's doing fine."

"Who is that?" Kaiya called out from the bathroom door where she had gone to freshen up after they had come into the apartment.

Kalilah told her it was Finn.

"Tell him I said hi," Kaiya said before going to her bag to pull out the blue dress she'd bought for their supper date tonight.

"I'm not a messenger," she tossed back at her sister.

"Hello?" Finn said, his tone uncertain and she'd almost forgotten he was still on the call.

"I'm still here."

"So, supper tonight?"

Typical male, pretending like he hadn't heard a word she'd said – or was he secretly hoping to make her resolve waver?

"I can't tonight, Finn." The next thing she heard was a click.

Kaiya's phone began ringing from across the room. Her sister glanced at the screen with a mischievous look before she said.

"It's Finn." She lifted the phone up to her ear. "Hello," she started tentatively, and two seconds into the call and she was giggling. Finn made her sister laugh? Just great. She'd been trying to make Kaiya laugh all day but hadn't succeeded, and now she was chuckling at whatever Finn was saying. He wasn't even that funny in her opinion.

She tried to ignore Kaiya's side of the conversation by scrolling through Instagram. Kalilah could still hear her sister's laughter and it annoyed her. She slumped on the bed in exhaustion, thoroughly disgusted at the ways that man got to her without even trying.

"Here," the voice jolted her from indignant thoughts. Kaiya leaned over her, offering the phone.

"What do you want Finn?"

"You. Us," his tone was serious. "But I know you're not ready for that yet." He placed emphasis on yet. "Anyway, your sister doesn't mind if I hang out with you girls tonight." He sounded smug.

Of course Finn would find a way to charm his way in. The man had two ways of getting what he wanted: Either muscle, as in by sheer force of will and strategic planning, or by turning on the charm. Something few people could resist, and her sister obviously couldn't either. She explained to him that it was an all-girls affair and that she didn't want him there.

"Well, I've been invited," he said in a calm manner that made her want to hurl the phone at the nearest hard surface. *Good God!* How had she gone from saying no to wanting to tear her own hair out?

"You're a good actor, I'm sure you can come up with an excuse to not make it. So un-invite yourself," she hissed in a low tone. She didn't want her sister hearing her.

"Don't be mean, Kalilah, I already said he could come!" Kaiya piped from across the room, loud enough for Finn to overhear it.

"I'll meet you girls in the hotel lobby," he replied confidently, and rang off before she could say anything else.

Kalilah hurled the phone at the bed, with enough force to make it bounce, before falling back.

She looked up at her sister's quirked eyebrow and wanted to throttle her for inviting him.

"What was that look for?" Kaiya was obviously amused.

"You know why," Kalilah offered. "I didn't want to have supper with him."

"You could have filed for the annulment in Seattle, you know, and had the lawyers battle it out," her sister pointed out.

"And miss the look on their faces when I walked away a free woman? Never!" she joked, knowing that her sister was perfectly correct in her assessment. Jonathan had given her the very same argument, but she felt the need to come here and face Finn. She wanted him to see the woman she'd become. The woman who could no longer be pressured into doing anything that she didn't want to do. Now here she was being pressured into dinner.

"I had almost forgotten about that quirky sense of humor of yours," Kaiya said.

"Seriously though, I wanted to do this personally. I had to come and look them in the eyes while I avenged that part of me that was betrayed all those years ago." She didn't need to explain who *they* were.

Her sister moved around the bed to hug her at that declaration and smiled sadly.

"If anyone can understand that, it's me."

Kalilah sighed and began explaining the bargain she struck with her husband.

Kaiya patiently and waited till the very end to comment.

"Does Jonathan know about this?"

"No, and frankly I'm unsure about whether or not I should tell him."

"I don't think you should," Kaiya advised her.

At that, Kalilah's eyebrows rose in astonishment.

"Don't tell him; he'll never understand. Imagine finding out that your girlfriend has to date her husband in order to get a divorce." Kalilah's stomach knotted at her sister's interpretation of her dilemma.

"So you're saying I should lie to my boyfriend?"

"Not a lie, more of an omission," she reassured.

She went over what her sister just said and realized that she may be right. It wasn't like Jonathan was in Montréal. He wouldn't find out unless she told him, and she didn't want him to get hurt either. This was her fight, and she was only doing what was necessary for their future.

"Maybe you're right."

"I know I am. After you're happily married to him with a baby, tell him then," she said baby in a hoarse whisper and then took a deep breath and cast her eyes down. She then shook off whatever she was feeling and continued, "so it doesn't come back to bite you in the butt." Kaiya advised on a devious wink.

Kalilah's mind was blown.

"Wow, I can't believe I'm getting this kind of advice from you... my baby sister."

"I'm not a baby anymore." Kaiya laughed at her incredulous face and stuck out her tongue at her.

"You're my baby. Do you remember when you snuck into my bedroom during the night when you had nightmares or believed you had a monster living in your closet?"

"Hey! The monster was real, I saw him." She gave Kalilah a small shove. "You always protected me, even though Mother would be upset to find us in the same bed in the mornings." Her tone turned serious and then she continued, "Listen, sis, I was too young to help you back when Dad threatened you, but I'm older now and ready to help you get your happily ever after, on your terms. And as for Finn?"

"What about him?" Kalilah asked, choked up. She was so moved by her sister's declaration.

"It's just one night, and you can totally spend it driving him crazy."

"What did you have in mind?"

"Don't worry about it, I have a plan."

***

For a woman who was always upfront about her emotions, Kalilah was already feeling defeated. Even as she listened to her sister's plan, Kalilah wondered how moments of passion and indifference were going to get her the annulment papers in three months.

But did she voice even a single complaint? No, Kalilah was a sucker for her sister's smile, and for the look on her face when she pulled out the shimmering floor-length gold sheath with a slit up to one thigh. She knew that she was going ahead with this plan, if for no reason than to appease her sister.

Her only input she had was on the makeup. She wanted it to be as simple as possible, and after a while Kaiya agreed. After Kaiya got dressed in a thigh-length, white, sequined dress, they went down to the lobby in an elevator where her big-headed, annoying, arrogant, over-the-moon sexy, soon-to-be-ex-husband was waiting for them.

Finn looked devilishly handsome in his back tux. It was molded to his muscled body. His dark hair was slicked back, and he looked like the man she fell in love with years ago. Finn's reaction when he caught sight of her was satisfying and comical in equal bounds. Kalilah had never left a man speechless before. Many had commented on her beauty, at least Finn and Jonathan had, so had her girlfriends, but she had never had a man stare at her and swallow only to stare again. His heated stare overwhelmed her and made her feel vulnerable. She broke the silence when they neared.

"Hello, Finn."

***

If he thought she was a hurricane in his office, he clearly didn't know what he was thinking. She was an act of God the same way a rainbow or a volcanic eruption was a natural phenomenon, and there was no understanding its mysteries. One minute she was subdued, and the next she was a fire that dared a bold soul to reach for her flames.

The dress was pure sex, with the promise of hot passion and mystery. Sexy, erotic without being vulgar – but it made a lot of promises in between the lines. Such marvelous line too.

The gold material clung to her body, showcasing her subtle curves, long lines that were not marred by the presence of underwear (he knew that much, unless it was a thong and even that was much... more) before it flowed down in long lines to her feet. It was completely modest, subtle, and even mysterious until one caught sight of glistening flesh from a slit in the skirt that reached her thigh and was hidden in the long folds until she moved.

And what a move, a sinuous stretch of a toned body that held the eyes, stole the senses, and built a desire that he knew would be impossible to quench if he didn't have her.

He had thought he had the upper hand, but he was quickly disabusing himself of that notion. He had never begged for a dinner invitation; worse still, he had never had his own invitations turned down. And, to add salt to the injury, he had invited himself by underhanded means, only to have his victory thrown in his face.

Judging from the glances in their direction, he wasn't the only man tempted by the vision she presented. Men were casting subtle and obvious glances in their direction and Kalilah? The little minx was enjoying the show.

He scowled and he saw that she stared at him skeptically.

"You girls look beautiful. Ready to head in?"

"Let's go." Kaiya broke in. "I'm starving!"

The pleasure of leading two beautiful women to dinner was dimmed by the fact that none of them belonged to him.

Moments later the sisters each linked their arms into one of his, and they were led to their reserved table. Dinner passed in a flurry of chatter between him and Kaiya. They mostly discussed the best locations for her dance school. Kalilah remained silent at the table, sipping on cocktails, and only answered any questions in a monotone.

Finn and Kaiya had tried to pull her into their conversation, but she remained silent. She spoke more to the waiter than she did to him and Kaiya. Finn would be lying if he said it didn't bother him. He wished she would say something – anything. They talked so much at brunch, and he was hoping that it would be the same tonight.

If Kalilah smiled at their personal waiter one more time, he wasn't going to be responsible for his actions. He spied the young, overblown, dark-haired man approach, and he scraped his chair back with a force that had people from other tables looking their way. He was damned if he was going to sit back and allow another man to ask his wife to dance or even make her smile.

He had ignored the jazz band long enough, and the men who had eyes for his wife had taken it as permission to approach. Somewhere, in the recesses of his mind, a voice tried to remind him she was intent on becoming his ex. He wouldn't be entertaining such thoughts. Not today. Not ever. He would woo his runaway wife if it was that last thing he did.

***

"Let's dance." She looked from Finn's proffered hand to her sister's smirking face and knew she wasn't going to be any help.

She tried though.

"I can't leave..."

"Please, don't let me stop you. Enjoy yourselves!" Kaiya stalled her excuse with a flashy smile.

Gone was the innocent face and its place was a pixie, a mischievous imp. She would have enjoyed the transformation a whole lot more if wasn't directed against her. With no more excuses available to her, she placed her hand in his offered one and allow him to lead her closer to the band.

He held her close and Kalilah allowed him. It had been a long time since she danced. His masterful hands led her, but still allowed her freedom to make her body move in all the ways it wanted to. She breathed in his scent and sighed. He smelled really good. She could almost get lost in the scent. He twirled her and she went willingly. The skirt of her dress twirled by the sudden motion and exposed a bit more flesh but she didn't notice. He did. A few eyes widened in appreciation at the show, and he pulled her body back to him as he silently vowed, no more twirls.

"I missed this."

"This?"

"Dancing like this… with you." Kalilah's confession startled her and she decided that the alcohol she had earlier had inebriated her. She remembered how they would dance like this when her parents threw soirees at the estate. They would sneak away, to another part of the house where they could still hear the music, and sway together.

He held her tighter and said "I missed you too babe," against her ear.

She only looked up at him for a brief second and turned her head away to fix it on a point over his shoulder. She decided to not respond to what he said. There was no point in repeating herself. The reasons why she couldn't stay were so obvious, starting with him and ending with her new life in Seattle. Many miles away.

"Guess what else I missed?"

"Kissing me?"

Lilah snapped her head back at that and her brown eyes settled on his lips. She licked her lips and averted her glance then.

"No, my sister. I missed her so much. I didn't know how much until I saw her and how much she's grown up. She was about fifteen when I left, and now she's twenty," she stated ruefully.

"Five years is a long time, of course she changed. We all changed."

Kalilah sighed at the tone and allowed herself to sway in a slow circle, her hand resting lightly on his shoulder. She could get lost in his embrace if she wasn't careful. Everything about him intoxicated her.

"She's changed so much that she's almost a stranger, but then she does something and I see remnants of the sister I knew."

"She's changed a lot, especially after she came back from New Brunswick, but not in a negative way."

"She seems older somehow, like she has more wisdom or something."

He agreed with her observation, a bit of guilt driving him.

"Did my parents say why she went away to boarding school? It just seems so unlike them to send her so far away from their reach."

"Your parents were pretty evasive about that, but they finally confided that she was having a hard time at school and hanging around 'a degenerate', so they thought it best that she went away for a while." He shrugged, and Kalilah rolled her eyes.

***

"I think I know what I want to do while I'm waiting."

"Waiting…?" The change of topic was abrasive when all he was really following was the movements of her body. He allowed his hands to gently roam her back.

128

"For the annulment."

He winced at that reminder. He didn't want to think about an annulment, not when his arms were wrapped around her. Mine! Of course, he sounded like a barbarian, but he didn't particularly care.

"What would you like to do?"

"I want to find a volunteer position, maybe at a shelter, or any organization that offers services to women who are at risk."

"That's a terrific idea." Good. He hoped that if she built a strong enough base here, she'd want to stay and not return to Seattle.

"I think so too, it's time I gave back to the community I grew up in," she smiled.

"Then you should do it and, like I told you before, if you need anything let me know. I'll help in any way that I can."

"I'll keep that in mind."

He tugged her even closer to his chest. He wished he could kiss her and touch her in all the places lovers touched each other. He wondered what would happen if he moved his hand a little lower. Would she get spooked and bolt from his arms, or allow him to continue the gentle exploration? They continued to dance slowly, Finn all the while wishing he could have more liberties with her.

"I'll have to find a condo. Hotels are nice, but they're not suited for everyday living."

"What if I find you a condo? You can have one of my newly-built, fully-furnished condos tonight."

"I want the opportunity to find my own place."

"As you wish then," he trailed off at that point. "I think you're doing a good thing, sharing your strength of will with people who need assistance. It's a lot to take on, and I think you're incredible for doing it. Not everyone is as empathetic, or even cares as much as you do."

"Thanks for saying that." She smiled. His heart soared.

"You don't have to thank me. I am damn proud of you and your accomplishments. Don't forget to take some time out for yourself, though. Being around too much sadness can take a toll," he advised. She looked up into his eyes, her dark eyes turning light.

"Thanks Finn." They continued staring into each other's eyes for a while until she relented and averted her now sad gaze, breaking their eye contact.

Damn propriety, Finn dragged her by the hand and away from the dance floor. They stepped out of the restaurant and into the balcony hidden by long curtains that effectively shielded them from prying eyes. It was empty as well.

"Tell me: what's going on?"

***

The light from inside provided the balcony with a soft intimate glow. She turned to face Finn and could see the concern etched on his face. She instantly regretted her behavior at dinner. He'd done nothing but sing her praises since they'd last met and she was a brat during supper. Granted, she was salty about him inviting himself, but it was no reason to be rude.

"I'm sorry about my behavior during dinner."

He told her that she didn't need to apologize for that and asked that she tell him the reason she had suddenly become sad.

"I'm just worried about my sister. I can tell she's been through something and I would like the chance to make up for not being there for her."

"I'm sure your sister will appreciate it, but listen to me babe: You can't be hard on yourself. You have your own issues to deal with and I'm positive your sister understands that. If she didn't, she wouldn't be spending so much time with you now." He was right she knew, but the guilt still ate at her.

"She seemed happy tonight, didn't she?" She asked him.

"She seemed in good spirits, plus I really did enjoy our dinner conversation."

"I noticed."

They remained in comfortable silence for a bit until she finally said, "Anderson sisters. Screwed up by their parents.

Doomed from birth to always be used by them. They sacrificed their first daughter and God only knows what they did to the second."

"There was no sacrifice," he responded trying to convince her.

Of course he would defend them. "Have you forgotten that I had no say in the direction of my life?"

"I loved you Lilah. I still do. I had always planned on getting married to you and it wasn't for any other reason except solely for love. Your father found out about our relationship; I don't know how he did, but he had called me for a meeting and asked me if we were seeing each other, I told him that not only were we in love but I would propose to you soon. At the time I thought he would fire me or tell me to stay away from you, however he told me how pleased he was his business would remain in the family and that after our wedding he'd give me the position of COO of the company. I agreed with the offer simply because I wanted to be able to provide for my wife after our wedding."

"Really?" she asked coldly.

"Yes really. We were in love and I wanted to make you mine in every sense of the word."

"That doesn't make sense. I heard my father say that you would get the company after you married me." She answered airily without bothering to look at him. She moved to the balcony railing and leaned against it lightly as she looked at the city's light shimmering over the water. *Could all of what he'd just said be the truth?* Did she disrupt their lives over her own misunderstandings? She didn't want to admit defeat.

"After I told him that I loved you and would marry you," he insisted.

She couldn't believe it. She refused to think about what his words could mean if this was in fact true.

***

"Was it so bad marrying the man you were in love with?" As soon as he said the words, he realized he didn't want to know the answer.

"It was hell in the beginning after we got married. You know for a while I couldn't believe that you would use me to get what you wanted. I had never hated a person as much as I hated you on our wedding day and then the days, weeks and months that followed." She returned calmly and that scared him. He couldn't believe she loathed him that much. He was also aware that she didn't say years.

"Kalilah." His voice was slightly raised in a warning.

"No, I need to get it off my chest."

"Go ahead," he offered and waited for the blows to land.

They fell with expert aim. "I hope it's been enough Mister COO, I hear all about your work and how well you handle the company you got as a dowry for marrying the first Anderson daughter. I hope it has satisfied you."

That last dig proved too much for him. He was standing over her, without remembering how he had crossed the distance from across the balcony. "Satisfaction? No, I haven't felt it in a long time." He growled incensed while brushing his fingers against her exposed brown shoulder that complimented the color of her dress.

"Let go of me this minute!"

"Listening to you speak makes me think that I've been cheated; I got the company according to you, but not the first Anderson daughter. It's about time I remedy that." The words came from somewhere inside of him that was tired of being falsely accused of something that didn't happen the way she thought it did. Time to show his wife who she really belonged to.

"What do you think you're doing?"

He looked down into her eyes and he couldn't see a hint of fear. Her mouth said one thing but her eyes they were saying something different to him.

"Too bad I wasn't asking for permission," he answered with a slow grin that warned her of his intentions much too late. She raised her hand to slap him but he caught it on the upward swing and easily twisted her hand behind her back, effectively pushing her up against him with her breasts heaving and her anger written on her face.

He took a long look at the picture she presented. Chest heaving, eyes lit with anger, head tilted up in defiance. She looked so alluring, so beautiful, and he knew he had to taste her lips. His head descended. At first it was punishing, with her straining close-mouthed against him, his hands running slowly over her shoulders and along her arms. He explored slowly with unsettled fingers. He wanted to do more than he already was. His head throbbed with the ache and desire that clouded his mind.

She suddenly began to move her lips beneath his.

***

It was a kiss to end all kisses, his lips slid over hers in a languid move taking his time to tease, his was a masterful touch. She'd never felt such intense passion with anyone except him. The hands that had held hers captive released, and brushed up her body in one long stroke. She moaned into his mouth at the invasion. Her hands instinctively travelled up his muscled torso until they encircled his neck. The hairs at his nape were soft and smooth. Her mouth eased open, allowing him to take advantage of her parted lips, and he used his skillful tongue to invade her mouth and explore her taste.

Liquid heat travelled throughout her body, her entire being flooding with desire. Her hands were twisted in the material of the black tux at his shoulder and she was strained against him – wanting more, needing more. Finn backed her up against the wall and his hand reached even lower.

He broke the kiss and said, "I've been tortured by the view of your smooth skin all night, and I am intent on finding out if it's as soft as it looks."

Before she could even think to respond, he bent his head and started a trail of kisses down her throat as his hand reached through the slit in her dress and trailed upwards. She raised her leg and parted her thighs to accommodate his exploration. His hand brushed softly at one expanse of skin then another, and she moaned at those teasing touches. She wanted him to ease the desperate ache that had formed between her thighs.

She moaned again when his fingertips skimmed over her mound.

"No underwear?" he asked, shocked, as he took a step back to look into her eyes.

"It wouldn't work with this dress," she said, and pressed her body closer to his.

He pressed his fingers onto her sensitive flesh and she pushed her hips forward, wanting more.

"Please." Her voice sounded distant to her ears.

A sudden roar of sound had them jolting apart. They were both breathing hard. It took a few minutes for her breathing to return to normal and for her strewed thoughts to rearrange themselves. When it did, the realization of what she had done shocked her. *God!* How could she have lost her mind so quickly, so completely? This was Finn, the man she hated, her soon to be ex-husband. Her body had no such problem; it wanted nothing more than to go back into his arms and continue where they stopped. He seemed to have sensed her thoughts and took a step in her direction.

She took a step back.

"No, we can't." With that, she fled the cloud of passion on the balcony.

CHAPTER 8

KALILAH AWOKE WITH A START as the rays of the morning sun filtered through the drapes.

It had been a week since the night she'd kissed Finn, and it was still heavy on her mind. She didn't know how it was possible, but her lips still tingled anytime she thought of it, and her nerves were buzzing with electricity when she thought about his sensual touches. She couldn't believe that she had allowed Finn to get so close to her. She didn't know what had come over her, but she had gotten so lost in the frenzy of his touch.

The kiss reminded her so much of how it used to be between them. It had rendered her totally unaware of anything else except the two of them in that moment – until the noise from inside had filtered out onto the balcony, forcing them apart. Her heart sped at the implications of what would have taken place if they weren't interrupted. She'd rushed away from the balcony after the haze of desire had ebbed and the realization of what she had done sank in. She'd grabbed Kaiya's hand and sent Owen a quick text to meet her outside.

They had slid into the car and Owen had pulled off as if he knew she was fleeing something dangerous. Even as she thought about it, she knew that she wouldn't have been able to stop herself from being completely taken by Finn in every sense of the word, and she didn't know how to feel about that. She'd been ignoring Finn all week and trying not to think about the kiss.

For that reason, she'd applied for multiple volunteer positions, and had scrolled through the company's real estate site searching for her perfect temporary home.

She placed the memories of the kiss in the back of her mind, and turned over in her bed. Kaiya was still asleep in the bed next to hers, one pillow tucked between her legs and another under her head.

Her phone chirped from her bedside table at that moment and she ignored it. She had a strong feeling that it was Jonathan texting to wish her a good morning, and she figured she'd respond to his message later. She felt too much like a fraud at the moment. She also wondered if what Finn had said was the truth. Was it possible that she misunderstood Finn's side of things? She didn't want to think about that now. She had Jon to consider. She needed to confess.

She mobilized her limbs and got up from the bed, being careful not to rouse her sister from sleep, and tiptoed into the washroom. Once inside, she brushed her teeth and then discarded her clothes. After that was done, she hopped into the shower and took her time lathering up. The feel of the water against her skin did little to wash away the guilt of betraying Jon.

The worst part of it all was that she wanted to kiss Finn again. But she would never admit that aloud. That would be her own little secret. She felt like the worst human being ever.

Here she was with the sweetest man on the face of the Earth, and she was fraternizing with her husband. *Ex-husband.* She knew at that moment that she couldn't allow a kiss between her and Finn to happen again. It was bad enough to be married with a boyfriend, but to cheat on your boyfriend with your husband – that was beyond her. What a complicated mess. She would need to tell Jonathan about that kiss. It was the right thing to do, no matter the consequences.

***

After their passionate encounter on the balcony, Finn had deliberately stayed away from Kalilah. He wanted to give her time to think about everything he had told her. After telling her the truth, he'd seen the uncertainty in her eyes. She still didn't believe him, and it hurt, but if the passion that had flared between them was any indication, he still had a chance.

He could still taste her. He traced his fingers along his lips and felt his entire body shudder, just as he had when they had shared that steamy kiss on the balcony. Her lips tasted as good as a fine wine allowed to age, probably better if he were being honest. He wasn't sure if the distance and time that had passed between them was to blame for how much more enticing her lips tasted.

Her response to him was thrilling; she had kissed him without much fight and had submitted herself to the passion that was theirs alone. He had managed to bring down some of her walls, but he needed to break them down completely. He needed full access to her mind and heart.

Now here he was, standing before her door, bearing gifts with genuine hope of finally resolving the issues before them. Finn just couldn't wait any longer and he rammed the door three times with his folded fist. He'd sent her a text earlier, and she'd never responded. Getting back to the place they used to be wouldn't be easy, but it would be worth it.

The door slowly swung open, and with it came the startled, wide eyes of Kaiya. She eyed him with some degree of shock, but his charming demeanor – accompanied with a perfectly executed smile – brought one to her face too.

"Finn!" She sounded surprised. He could tell that she'd just woken up. Her messy hair was piled on top of her head, and her nightgown was crooked.

He greeted her and placed a kiss on each of her cheeks as she invited him inside.

"Is that breakfast?" Kaiya asked.

He handed her the bagels and coffee he'd gotten from a café near his apartment.

"It smells so good." She took his offering and brought it to the table.

***

After she was done with the task of cleaning her body, she turned off the spray and stepped out of the shower. She dried herself quickly. She heard voices in the other room, which meant Kaiya was up and probably watching television. She would ask her to accompany her to lunch. She grabbed a pair of underwear from the nearby drawer and put it on. As an afterthought, she put on a robe before stepping out of the bathroom.

Thank God she put on the robe, because the sight of the person standing in the suite, speaking to her sister, stunned her.

"What are you doing here?" Her sister and Finn both turned toward her. They had obviously not heard when she came into the room.

"Good morning sunshine," His mouth formed a wide smile and she saw his perfect white teeth. Almost immediately her mind drifted back to the kiss they shared. She scrapped the thought when he spoke again. "You're not ready yet?"

The confusion must have shown on her face because he said, "Didn't you get my text?"

She told him that she didn't receive his text, not bothering to inform him that she had been ignoring her phone, too afraid to face the music.

"No matter, I brought gifts," he pointed to the bagels on the table and then continued, "and I also wanted to take you out for lunch." She regretted not checking on her phone when it chirped. If she had received the text earlier, she would have swiftly declined his invitation for lunch, hence saving her from having to face him.

"I'm sorry that you came all this way for nothing, but I have to decline." She tried to sound as genuine as possible, since she wasn't sorry.

"I won't take no for an answer. In fact, I'm prepared to sit in this room all day long and if you decide to leave this room, I'll follow you wherever you go." He sounded serious.

"I think I'll go take a shower now and leave you two to talk," said Kaiya as she took large steps toward the bathroom. Kalilah had totally forgotten about her sister being in the room with them. Before her sister closed the bathroom door, she stuck her head out and added, "Oh, and Lah? I have a lunch date with Jalissa, so don't worry about me." Kalilah gave her sister the evil eye before Kaiya slammed the bathroom door shut. Her sister knew her so well. She knew that Kalilah would use her as an excuse to not have lunch with Finn.

"Okay, fine."

"Don't try escaping through the window."

She rolled her eyes. Highly improbable since she was in the penthouse suite.

"Out!" Since he stood just outside the suite's bedroom, she slammed the French doors in his face.

She dressed quickly – not because she didn't want to keep him waiting, because she did. She was famished and was ready to put some food in her system. She threw on a pair of jeans, a yellow floral crop top and a pair of gold sandals. She added some Chapstick to her lips, wrapped her hair in a high bun, grabbed her purse, and then headed to the sitting area to meet Finn.

The lunch date went better than she thought it would. They had Owen drive them to Old Montréal since they didn't want to have to look for parking. The car ride to the old port was quiet. They were each stuck in their thoughts, but she sensed it every time Finn looked her way. She tried to not look back, and kept her focus outside the window. She was thinking of ways to tell Jonathan about the kiss between her and Finn – she finally decided to keep it a secret, along with everything else.

This trip home was making her into something she was not. A liar.

By the time they entered the restaurant and were seated in booths in the back, thoughts of Jon disappeared from her mind, as well as the possibility of Finn having never betrayed her in the first place. They ordered their meals, and Finn explained to her that a close friend of his owned the place. The restaurant itself was rustic, and gave off a romantic atmosphere with discreet lighting. When the waitress brought over their water, she was pleased to see paper straws. Finn was shocked by her delight over the straws, and she explained to him the importance of paper straws and the negative effects of plastic straws on the environment.

"You continue to surprise me, Lilah. Not only do you care for people, but you care for our environment as well."

She simply responded, "I do my part." The waitress brought over their meals, and Kalilah quickly dug into hers. The lobster she ordered was divine.

"About the kiss..." he started.

She shook her head and feigned ignorance.

"What kiss?" she asked, reaching for the juice atop the table.

Finn halted her action and managed to graze his fingers over her hand, making it tingle. He needed to stop touching her.

"Don't be daft. You know what kiss I'm talking about."

Kalilah raised her hand to cut him off and placed her fork onto the plate before she cleared her throat.

"Oh, that kiss. Let's not make a huge deal about it. It was nothing." Even as she said it, she knew it was a lie. That kiss was everything.

Finn took her hands in his and said, "That kiss meant everything to me; it gave me hope for us. You can't say you didn't feel the connection. I felt my wife in those lips, and if we weren't interrupted…"

"It's a good thing we were interrupted. It kept us, me, from doing something I would have regretted." She saw the scowl on his face, but didn't care. "Can you please do me a favor?"

"Anything except deny the connection that I felt with you during that kiss."

"Can we not talk about it?"

"I will cease talking about it as long as you make the effort to enjoy yourself on our dates. What do you say?"

She agreed, so after lunch, when Finn took her hand and led her closer to the water, where the paddleboats were stationed, she didn't make a fuss. Old Montréal bustled with activity. She was sure that if Finn wasn't holding her hand she would have gotten lost in the crowd.

When they got close to where the paddleboats were stationed, she slipped her hand from his and made to put some distance between them.

"Last one to get to the boats is a rotten egg," Kalilah said over her shoulder, and then she took off in a sprint. She looked back once and saw that Finn was right behind her, and burst into giggles.

"You little cheat," Finn said when he caught up with her. He wrapped his arms around her tiny waist and pulled her against his chest.

"Take it back! I gave you fair warning." She continued to chuckle, and he couldn't help but join in her laughter.

"Some things never change," he said. In the past she had played this exact game with him many times, and he always caught her no matter the distance she'd have between them.

They walked the remainder of the distance holding each other's hand, like lovers taking a stroll. Luckily when they got to the kiosk, there wasn't a huge line. Finn paid for their paddleboat and they made their way to the water. After they got settled, another couple tried racing them, and they took on the challenge.

"Go faster, Finn!"

"I am going as fast as we can," he responded. They both laughed at the silliness of it all. In the end they got ahead of the other couple. They spent the next hour boating along the lake. Kalilah couldn't remember the last time that she'd had this much fun.

"I want to try ziplining," she said after they left the paddleboat station. She'd never ziplined before, and was curious about it.

Finn agreed and they went towards the ziplining station. They waited in the line for fifteen minutes before they got their turn. After getting harnessed, the guide asked if they wanted to ride together in the sweetheart position. She didn't want to do it alone. Seeing it from the ground made it seem easy, now being on the top and looking down, she didn't think she'd be able to make it.

"Sure," Finn answered, "but only if it's okay with my lovely wife." Both Finn and the guide turned towards her waiting for her response and she nodded her head in the affirmative. She was strapped to Finn, sitting astride him as they faced each other. She placed her arms around his neck and wrapped her legs around his waist. She wondered again why she wasn't uncomfortable with her present closeness to Finn.

They spent the rest of the afternoon trying out other activities at the old port, and Kalilah began to see Finn in a new light. The day felt like the early days of their relationship. It was as if nothing had changed, except everything had. She wasn't as trusting as she was before, and Finn? He was more determined than ever.

CHAPTER 9

TWO WEEKS LATER, KALILAH FOUND HERSELF
seated at the breakfast table in her new condominium. She
had finally found a condo that met all her short-term needs.
Finn had been there to help her finalize the rental agreement
with the agent, and she appreciated his support even though
she didn't ask for it.

He had complimented her on her choice of building and
location. Apparently, he lived a few blocks down from her.
They'd gone shopping for appliances and furniture together
several times. He had offered her his opinion when she
requested it. She bought most of her furniture from Ikea and
she loved the different wood pieces, however it was a pain in
the ass to assemble them. Kalilah had thought the idea of

putting together her own furniture would give her a sense of purpose.

That was not the case. All it did was make her want to pull out her hair. The three of them – Kalilah, Kaiya, and Finn – had stayed up past midnight trying to put the furniture together, until Finn had huffed in frustration and declared he would pay people to come over and do it. Kalilah didn't even oppose him. She was just relieved about not having to see another screw.

True to his word, four men showed up the following day, and put together all the furniture under the watchful eye of her husband.

Ex-husband. She needed to remember that.

Finn had frequented her thoughts lately, a result of them spending more time together. He had settled himself into most aspects of her life, and she didn't mind it; she liked his companionship. She would miss the gentle truce they'd managed, once she left.

He had taken her dancing last weekend. When he called, she was still apprehensive about everything that happened between them, but Finn was an expert in getting his way. He had even extended the invitation to Kaiya, but she had declined.

Allowing Kaiya to talk her into yet another daring dress was probably not the best idea. She had seen how he looked at her – like she was his last meal before he faced death. Despite his obvious lust for her, he had been a perfect gentleman. Finn had looked good as well, his white button-down shirt was rippled with his muscles. He looked good enough to snack on. Not that she wanted to.

Electric, that was her first and last thought about the night. She had expected a lounge, thinking maybe he wanted to recreate that night at the hotel, however the club was fast-paced. She had always thought Kaiya to be the better dancer in the family, but that night her body moved in ways that she didn't think possible. He told her about the goings-on with his family. Apparently, his mom and younger sister were YouTube vloggers. Kalilah had created a Google account almost immediately and subscribed to their channels; she was loving his mom's food prep vlogs. Finn's family was always flamboyant – a total opposite to hers.

"Did I ever tell you that Alexandre isn't my biological dad?" Finn asked her as they lounged in the VIP section of the club. She thought she heard him incorrectly.

"Did you just say that Alexandre isn't your dad?"

"He is my dad, he just isn't the one who impregnated my mom." Kalilah was shocked, to say the least. She never knew that about him, and had asked him if he had ever met his biological father. Finn had simply told her that he had no interest in finding the man or getting to know him. Kalilah didn't know what to make of his curt tone and had changed the topic. They spent the remainder of the night dancing; Finn at her back while she grinded into him.

The thought of it now warmed her cheeks. She had loved the feel of his arms around her. Finn did nothing that she didn't want to. When she made the move and kissed him while they danced facing each other, it had shocked him – and her, honestly. The kiss started out soft, but quickly turned into something wild and insatiable. His warm fingers had stroked her body, and euphoric shivers made her quiver for more. The kiss was finally broken when someone bumped into them as the Electric Slide started to play.

They spent the remainder of the night dancing and sipping on cocktails until he brought her home. Her body still hummed with all the sensations from that kiss. She closed her eyes to banish her thoughts. Her phone chirped then, and she saw that she had received a new message.

It was from Jon, and it read *Missing you. Love you.* She sighed and sent him a quick *I miss you too* in return. It seemed that while her communication with Finn flourished, her communication with Jon dwindled, and she couldn't even blame the distance for it. It was her own guilt paralyzing her. She hated the idea of keeping things from him, especially considering how much she preached about honesty in relationships. Often, when he called, she would glance at the phone apprehensively before letting the call go to voicemail. And his tone when they did talk was often distracted. He questioned her on so many things that she wondered if he was spying on her. But that was impossible: when they Facetimed, she saw that he was at his apartment in Seattle.

She was a good person, well at least she was before she returned to her hometown. She never deliberately hurt anyone, so why was she in this complicated mess? Her emotions were all over the place. Recently, her heart seemed torn between two choices. On one hand, her heart was curious about exploring the desire that Finn stirred, and on the other hand was the safety she felt with Jonathan.

The realization that her heart might be the one to break came with an overwhelming ache that pressed so heavily it threatened to crush her chest. Kalilah rubbed a palm to the phantom ache in her chest, and looked up to catch her sister's smirking face, focused completely on her. Her sister had moved in with her after she got her new place.

"Something hurts?" Kaiya asked without a lick of concern on her face. In fact, the mockery was so heavy it demanded Kalilah's attention.

"Shut up."

Kaiya laughed off the warning as she scrambled off her chair to sit in front of the TV, her coffee mug in tow. Kalilah picked a bagel from Boulangerie, such delightful pastry was treated as the ambrosia of culinary delight by most people who ate it, but Kalilah tore off a piece then continued to mutilate it.

"If you're done playing serial killer on that bagel, can I have the remaining edible ones?" Her sister interrupted her thoughts with a knowing smile, and Kalilah contemplated throttling her.

Kalilah glared at her sister before launching the entire box at her. Kaiya only snatched it from the air with the deftness of an athlete and grinned at her spoils.

"You're going to get fat with all that junk that you eat while parked in front of the TV."

Kaiya shrugged.

"I'm almost skin and bones as it is. I would welcome some extra pounds," came the quick retort, followed by a low moan of delight as she bit into a pastry.

Kalilah threw her hands up in exasperation before tilting her cup to her lips. She frowned at the taste of the lukewarm liquid. She liked her coffee burning hot or ice cold, no in-between.

"What are you up to today?"

"I got a response from that job you told me about. They want me to come in later today with my photo ID. I really hope I won't need a valid health insurance card for this position." She had her old card, but it was expired, and since she wasn't planning on staying for more than six months, she didn't see the point of going through the process of getting a new one.

"Fingers crossed, then."

Kalilah carried her cup to the sink and rinsed it. Her alarm had ticked off at 5am, just when she was about to get some semblance of sleep. Owen, her faithful chauffeur, had delivered the bagels to her doorstep. It had become a habit for him. Always making sure she had her fancies every other morning. She didn't even bother getting another cup, even though she was still feeling groggy.

Kalilah plopped down on the couch, hard enough to scatter the nest of cushions Kaiya had set up around her, and it earned her a glare.

"I see you're determined to be a thorn in my side."

"Puh-lease!" Kalilah snorted down at her and looked at the screen diverted her attention "I know better than to bother you when Jude Law is right in front of you, I swear you lose all control of yourself."

"I do not," Kaiya feigned annoyance.

"You're practically drooling."

"Shut up," she retorted, and launched a pillow at her sister. Kalilah rolled as far as she could and snagged her own cushion as she escaped. She launched it at her sister, then quickly picked up another to bop her on the head with considerable strength.

Squeals, screams, and threats tore the morning calm apart. Anyone who opened the door would find the two girls, all grown up – but then, that was debatable from the way they were acting – having a vigorous pillow fight. Kaiya was racing in circles, launching multicolored cushions with careless aim that had them landing in every direction, while Kalilah was in hot pursuit and aiming more carefully. The two crashed in front of the TV, the elder tackling the younger and proceeding to tickle the snot out of her.

"Stop, just stop! Before I pee on myself," Kaiya said.

"Pheew! Proving to you who the boss is around here is hard work, Yellow, but someone has to do it," Kalilah exhaled in a noisy gust as she slid to the floor beside her sister.

"You cheated," Kaiya protested weakly.

"You're just saying that because you lost."

"You're just being a pain in my behind because your mind and your heart are at odds right now." Kaiya retorted. Kalilah winced and looked at her sister before looking away.

"That obvious, huh?"

"Only because I know you, silly."

"Good God, I should have just stayed away and returned after the annulment was finalized," she groaned.

"And miss all this?" Kaiya asked cheerfully.

"You're right, I definitely didn't want to miss showing you who is boss."

Kaiya stuck her tongue out at Kalilah.

"Seriously though, I'm glad you came home, no matter how much misery you think you're feeling. I'm happy you are here. I might sound selfish, but what's wrong with wanting to be happy? Sometimes you just gotta deal with what you've been served by fate. Considering everything you've learned since you've returned, I think you should definitely explore things with Finn. I don't want you to do something you may come to regret." Kaiya was on a roll.

"I still have Jon to consider. I don't want to hurt him."

Kaiya elected herself as the voice of reason.

"First of all, wouldn't it be better for both you and Jon if you sort through your feelings first, before fully committing to each other? You told me how sympathetic he was when you confessed your marital status to him. That speaks to how understanding he is as a human being. Secondly, you're married to Finn, and it's totally reasonable for you to want to make sure that there are no lingering issues between you two."

She thought of everything her sister was saying, but was still uncertain as to how to proceed. It was true that Jon was understanding, but everyone had their limits. She'd known that coming back for the annulment would be difficult, and she had prepared herself for every ploy they would've thrown at her.

What she hadn't seen coming were the romantic feelings for Finn, feelings she thought she'd buried a long time ago.

It complicated things.

Her phone chirped and saved her from having to respond. Kalilah scrambled to find it before it stopped ringing. It was a message, from Jonathan. At her sigh, Kaiya leaned closer to look at the screen then burst out laughing.

"You're in deep shit."

"Oh, shut up," she retorted finally, as she scrambled to her feet and stomped out of the kitchen with her phone in hand. The strains of laughter followed her all the way to her room. Even the slammed door didn't cut it off completely.

CHAPTER 10

A COUPLE OF DAYS LATER...

Finn's reflection in the mirrors that lined the hallways in Kalilah's building showed a man who looked happier than he had felt in years. He felt like he'd just gotten a new lease on life. His blue eyes glowed with excitement over what his future with Kalilah held. It had been a few days since he saw his wife, and he missed seeing her smile. He pressed the buzzer for her door and waited.

The door swung open slowly and Kaiya's face came into view. Her eyes widened and she looked down at her watch.

"You're early," she said.

"I was in the neighborhood and decided to come over earlier." He looked past her shoulder and wondered if Kalilah was even there. "Hope I'm not disrupting anything."

She gave him a knowing smile and gestured for him to come inside. The condo was all white, and featured huge windows that allowed natural light into the interior. A large white flat-screen TV was bolted to the wall, and a large white sectional adorned the living room. A couple of silver throw pillows were strategically placed on the sofa. A glass center table sat on a faux fur rug in the center of the living room. The French doors to the left of the living room led to a balcony where Kalilah had placed a barbecue grill. He smiled at the memory from when he'd come over a few days ago, only to see her and Kaiya determinedly putting the grill together. Maybe it was the craving for barbecued chicken and ribs, but the girls put the grill together in under two hours while he observed. They didn't want his help, and he didn't oppose their decision because his attempt at putting together their IKEA furniture was a bust.

"You're not intruding. I was about to hop into the shower anyway. How many buildings are we going to see today?"

"I have three buildings lined up." He pulled out his tablet and started scrolling through the buildings that he'd picked out while Kaiya watched. "And if you don't like any of the ones I have lined up, we can always keep looking. I know how important this is to you and I want you to have the best."

"I'm so excited!"

He needed to know where his wife was, and he was about to ask Kaiya when she said, "Kalilah should be up in a minute. She's in the basement, in the gym." She smiled knowingly and then added, "You should go find her while I hop in the shower."

She didn't have to tell him twice. He left the condo and headed down to the basement.

***

"You never fail to surprise me babe." She had felt him before he even spoke. It was the following morning and after another night of restless thoughts she decided she needed a good workout. She threw another punch at the training bag.

"My classmate Cassi introduced me to this when I moved to Seattle. It helped build my focus and mental strength. The physical endurance is a bonus."

Being in a new city and going through heartbreak had forced her to look into different ways to redirect her focus. She'd tried yoga, since so many people spoke of the mindful benefits, however she ultimately found the slow, mindful pace boring. It did nothing but make her think about Finn and how much she missed him. She'd stopped going to her yoga classes after two weeks. One day, while in class, she'd mentioned how boring and slow she found yoga to be, and her classmate Cassie mentioned that her boyfriend was a kickboxing instructor, and that Kalilah should look into it. She was unsure at first, but after meeting with Derrick, Cassie's boyfriend, and learning the fundamentals – as well as getting a few practices in – she fell in love with the sport.

A kickboxing routine required focus on one's energy, which allowed each practitioner to execute each punch and kick steadily and successfully. It also helped that it built her mental strength and physical endurance. She had hired Derrick as her personal trainer, and every time she had the urge to call Finn or felt the familiar heart pangs of missing him, she'd call Derrick for a session and would work out until her mind and heart changed their focus.

"Looking at you," his heated gaze roamed shamelessly over her body and she felt a congruous stir of excitement between her thighs, "someone may assume you're innocent or delicate, but you're anything but, aren't you, babe? You pack a mean punch."

She snorted.

"I've been looking to spice up my workout. Maybe I'll join you sometime for kickboxing."

She ignored what he said.

"I thought we were leaving at eleven am. You're early."

"I was in the neighborhood." He looked around the gym and then finally returned his gaze to her. She looked him over, and was impressed with what she saw. He was wearing a fitted black polo shirt that accentuated his body, as well as dark jeans and a pair of brand name sneakers. "This is a nice gym, seems well equipped with the latest workout machines."

"That was one of the main reasons I chose this condo over the others; its gym."

"Our company only offers the best," he responded, and she nodded her head. She wouldn't disagree on that fact. Her father's company owned the condo she leased.

"I should probably head up to get a shower. I'm starting to feel and look sticky."

Finn's stare became intense and unwavering, and she was grateful for her dark skin. If her skin was fair, it would turn bright pink under his stare, and she didn't know why... or did she?

"You look beautiful," he said finally. She unstrapped the mitts from her hands.

"Let's go up to my place. We need to leave soon anyway."

An hour later, the three of them piled up into Finn's white Mercedes. Kalilah sat in the front and Kaiya in the back, but the latter perched herself in the middle of the passenger seat. On the way to the first location, Kalilah received an email confirming that she had gotten the position at the shelter. She couldn't have been more excited, and she shared the good news with her companions.

"I'm so proud of you, sis! You deserve it."

"I'm proud of you as well; nothing beats doing what you love."

"Thanks! I'm just excited that I finally have something to keep me busy for the next few months." Finn was smiling, but after that proclamation his hold on the steering wheel tightened and the smile disappeared.

Kaiya didn't allow the tension in the car to remain. She chatted happily about the plans she had for her school, and soon all three of them were sharing ideas and giving their opinions. Kaiya suddenly changed the topic from her school, and instead asked if they remembered the time she'd caught them half-naked in the backyard. Both she and Finn tried to deny it had ever happened, but Kaiya insisted that it had.

She remembered that event like it was yesterday. It was after supper, and Kalilah had gone out under the guise of going for a walk. However, Finn was waiting for her at the very end of the garden, where it was mostly dark. They started making out almost immediately. The kiss had gotten so intense that they had both removed their shirts, wanting to feel more of each other. Just when things were really beginning to heat up, they heard laughter from behind them, and someone said, "I knew it!"

It was embarrassing for her sister to catch her in such an embrace, and she'd made Kaiya promise not to tell their parents. Her sister agreed to keep their secret, but only if Kalilah would lend her ID when she needed it. The little blackmailer.

She knew that her sister was trying to ease the tension between she and Finn by offering herself as their common enemy. In that moment, she loved her sister more than ever, and she was proud of the woman she was becoming. The car ride continued with Finn and Kalilah's continued denial of events, Kaiya laughing about all the times she had seen them sneaking away.

The first building that they visited was a bust. It was large and there was potential; however, it was a fixer-upper. Kaiya didn't want to have to deal with too many repairs.

The second was better than the first in that it was ready for immediate use, but it wasn't as roomy as Kaiya wanted it to be. Frustration was evident on Kaiya's face.

"I swear, they look so much bigger and nicer in the pictures," Kaiya muttered.

"We'll find something, sis. There's still one more we have to see, and it may work."

Finn suggested lunch, but Kaiya insisted on seeing the final location before succumbing to her hunger.

This building was closer to downtown, and could easily be accessed through the metro stations.

That was a plus for Kaiya.

Finn helped Kalilah out of the car, and never let his hand drop from her lower back. She didn't mind him holding onto her, either. Only because she felt as though she may pass out from hunger.

Kaiya's face nodded approvingly as she surveyed the building's surroundings. There were restaurants and shops, which would come in handy for parents when they dropped their kids off.

The street also seemed busy, which meant she would be able to market her school easily.

When they finally entered the building, it was larger than the first two buildings they saw. Wood floors ran throughout the building which was perfect. Kaiya moved forward excitedly, phone out, and then started to snap pictures of every corner of the building.

"Guys, I think this is it!" Kaiya shouted excitedly. "I was beginning to get worried."

"I told you we would find the perfect place. Did you doubt me?" Finn asked cockily.

"Thank you so much, I'll never doubt you again!"

Kalilah looked up at Finn, and she hoped her face showed the gratitude that she felt.

"Thank you," she mouthed.

He winked and gave her a bright smile.

"Kaiya is a tyrant; she would have continued from location to location until we all passed out from hunger."

She smiled at his feeble joke, not knowing how much that small act meant to him.

"Hey!" The shout startled them both but Kaiya was merely turning pirouettes. "It's perfect!" Her infectious good cheer filled the large room. "I can't wait to open it up to young aspiring dancers. World class dancers will be created here. You guys will be part of history," she said loftily, stretching her hands to encompass the entire room in a theatrical gesture… and promptly ruined the effect as her stomach rumbled.

"Kaiya, was that you?" Finn asked, lips twitching.

She burst into laughter as she guiltily admitted, "I might have been too nervous to eat breakfast."

"Thank God for lunch," he called as he ushered the two of them out. Kalilah had to drag her sister out of her dream location. Finn locked up, and took the two of them out to lunch.

CHAPTER 11

THREE MINUTES IS HOW LONG IT HAD TAKEN Finn's thoughts to bring Kalilah back to mind.

He put a hand to the knot that threatened to suffocate him and unraveled it in one tug, throwing the offending piece of fabric on his desk. He had donned a tie for the monthly office meeting, because he had a rule for corporate attire at work and he couldn't break his own rule.

He also had a rule about procrastination and lazing about, but he was going to break it today.

Thoughts of his wife kept driving through his mind. Wife. They were married and he intended to stay that way. He'd broken through a few of her walls already and he didn't even think she realized that fact. She had still not spoken about staying or dropping the annulment and it gave him some pause – made him uncertain of his next move.

For a man who was used to actions, who ran a multimillion-dollar company and had a bit of control issues, it was difficult to sit back and wait for her to realize what he already knew – that they belonged together. He couldn't lose her; couldn't allow her to get scared of the intensity of emotions they evoked in each other. The way he felt about her scared him, but losing her a second time scared him more.

He shouldn't have let her go so easily. He should have fought harder for her. Convinced her how wrong she'd been about him. His own uncertainties about her age and whether she was ready for a relationship had propelled him into working hard so he could excel in his career. He had lost so many valuable years with her because he didn't try hard enough. He didn't blame her for leaving, and never had. She did what she thought was right for her, and he was proud of her for taking a stand. However, sometimes he wished she'd had given him the chance to explain before she cut him off. He would have moved with her to Seattle if she had asked him to.

Nothing he could do to change the past.

She was right about one thing though; pushing this company to the top had not satisfied him. Day after day of relentless work and strategizing to stay one step ahead of the moneymaking game had not quenched the need that only she could fulfill.

He loved Kalilah with every atom of his being. There was nothing in this world he wouldn't do for her. It wasn't about the chemistry or lust between them. It was about the realization that he would do anything to be with her. If she asked him to move back to Seattle today, he would pack his bags in a hurry. He wanted to be wherever she was. He knew his life would not be worth living if he lost her again. He didn't even bother to dispute that thought – he knew it to be true.

The power that came with the money he'd made had served as a Band-Aid for the emptiness he felt. And it worked for a while – five years to be exact – and he thought he would be okay for a bit longer, but she had come into town and lit fires under him with a vengeance. The empty space was filling up slowly, but he wanted more. He needed his wife in every way.

The thoughts drove him from his chair and to the view of the city. Many days had been spent in front of this same view, contemplating life and the unexpected turns it could take. Come to think of it, he had stood in this same spot, idly regarding the distant sheen of water, many times, contemplating the rewards those unexpected turns could bring.

The times he'd spent with her since she'd been back were amazing. He hadn't felt so alive and happy for years. His life would not be much worth living if he lost her again. What they had between them was more, much more. Now he just had to convince her of that, too. He loved her. He wished his love alone was enough to make her stay. Even if she didn't feel this all-consuming love for him, he knew his love for her was enough to carry them both. Now he just had to convince her to tell him how she really felt about him.

Finn stalked out of the office like a man with a mission.

"Hello Lilah." She had just stepped onto the sidewalk after work when she heard the greeting. She looked up and saw Finn leaning against a black Rover, his feet crossed at his ankles. She was pleasantly surprised to see him there, and she didn't want to explore the reasons for that.

"Fancy seeing you here."

"I'm full of surprises," he returned just as smoothly.

"I bet. So, what brings you down here?" She knew the question was silly, since he obviously came looking for her.

"It's a surprise." He turned around, opened his front passenger door and said, "Come with me to find out."

She hesitated for a bit because she was exhausted from work and wanted to go home to rest, but she conceded and climbed into his car.

He took her to the circus.

Even though she had made him promise early on not to take her there, she was happy he took her anyway. He had taken her on every single adult-sized ride and a few kid-sized rides as well. There had to be something completely odd about having a businessman do an about-face and become fierce at the 'shoot to win a toy' booth. He was a passionate creature and she had been mistaken to think all that passion was being directed into business. Another side of him shone through – carefree, alive, barely-leashed passion, and laughter. The reality of that had dealt a severe blow to the image of him she had carried all these years. She stole looks at him when she thought he was not looking, and with every glance she liked what she saw. And that was what she was afraid of.

Was it the dizzying rides, or could she just plead guilty to having a sugar overload? Kalilah found herself enjoying her time with Finn. They watched a few performances by a clown, who gave her a balloon animal: she would cherish it forever. They also caught a performance by an acrobat and juggler. The performance that intrigued her the most was the one with the lions. She wondered how they had gotten the animals to "dance." She had so much fun, and it was all because of Finn.

Jonathan. She had to remind herself that she loved him, and her future was with him. She smiled when she looked over and caught Finn playing golf with a bunch of kids. He punctuated every swing with hilarious comments that had the children giggling.

He had won, too, but gave the kids the chance to pick up the plastic trophy. Much later, they walked back to the car and got in. Kalilah couldn't help but compare the man walking beside her to the man she met on her first day back in Montréal. This man was the one she had fallen in love with years ago. The man she still loved with all her heart.

"Is that a frown? I thought we had a good time."

He startled her with the comment.

"Yes." She thought of a quick excuse. "I was just thinking of all the work I have to do tomorrow."

"I wonder…?" he started. She was curious.

"What do you wonder?"

"If you're still as ticklish."

She backed away from him and pushed her body closer to the car's door not that it would do anything to help her if he decided to tickle her. Just then he raised his hand and a mischievous gleam came into his eyes.

"Don't you dare!"

"I won't, at least not here, I do have a sense of occasion."

She snorted.

"I suppose I should be grateful."

"How's work going so far?"

"I'm enjoying it, honestly, although it's a lot of work. I can't say anything negative."

"Don't over work yourself, babe."

"Today I had to turn away a nineteen-year-old girl because she had a dog. No dogs are allowed in the shelter since there are other clients who are allergic to them."

"That's unfortunate."

"I felt horrible having to tell her that we couldn't accept her if she had the animal. I was so saddened about the situation I had the client wait while I texted Kaiya and asked her to come over. I had Kaiya pay a hotel for this girl for three months. It's the least I could do, even though it isn't allowed."

"And that's all that matters, she'll have a warm bed and food to eat. That's a victory," he replied.

"Too small of a victory. What will happen to this girl after the three months are up? This girl needs continuous support." She felt crummy when the girl thanked her profusely. "It made me feel completely inadequate."

"You did your best, babe." he offered tentatively.

"That's not the best I can do." Finn glanced at her and away.

"What more can you do?" he asked genuinely curious.

"I wish I had my own shelter, so that I could provide services to people who are often overlooked by public agencies."

"I think it's a good idea, and like I said before I will help in any way that I can. If anybody can do this then it's you." His faith in her made her tremble.

"You really think so?"

"I know how passionate you are about helping others. So, you should do it. I may even have the perfect building for you. I just acquired it from a poker game. You should use it for something good."

Kalilah was shocked.

"Since when do you play poker?"

"Surprise."

The car slowed then came to a stop and Kalilah looked out to see that she was outside her condominium complex.

"I really had a good time today. Thank you for making me forget about my troubles even though it was only for a little while."

"My pleasure, babe."

CHAPTER 12

Kalilah entered her building and smiled at the doorman when he waved at her. She rejected the idea of exercise on the stairs for the cool efficiency of the elevator. She entered the elevator alone. She pressed the button that would bring her up to her floor and leaned against the wall. Right now, the soft rug under her feet was a whole lot of temptation, but Kalilah refused to crumble into the luxury. Considering her train of thought, skipping dinner was starting to look like a good idea. It had been two days since Finn had brought her to the circus, and she was happy for the reprieve.

Kalilah let herself into the condo and heard murmurs coming from the dining parlor. She ignored it. She was too exhausted to join polite conversation when her body demanded sleep. She stripped off her purse and coat and laid them on the first available flat surface before making a beeline straight for her room.

"Hello, angel." The voice had her quickly turning in shock.

"Jon? Jonathan!" Kalilah's eyes widened as a familiar body bounded over to her and trapped her in a bear hug. She was sure a few of her bones had been broken by the sheer force of that embrace.

"I missed you, angel." The gruff baritone surrounded her and cut off all thoughts.

"I missed you, too." *Did I?* She was still in shock, and in the haze of emotions coming to the surface, dismay was rising fast. She spied her sister over his shoulder. Kaiya gave her a pitiful stare, and Kalilah turned away, unwilling to allow the guilt to make her scramble out of his embrace. An embrace that used to make her feel warm and loved only served to make her feel smothered now.

He released her from the embrace and then grabbed her by the hand and dragged her toward the dining room. He deposited her in a chair and took a seat himself, but dragged his chair closer to hers. He then captured her hands within his.

"You're here. Wow!" *Was that her voice?* It sounded squeaky. In her defense the words just fell out of her mouth without input from her currently fried brain.

"You sounded so sad over the phone, and I missed you so much. That's why I decided to come cheer you up," he said with a smile and somehow, the gesture did not sound as romantic as it should have, as it would have before. Somehow, his travelling all the way from Seattle to 'cheer her up' was not something she cared for.

She would have preferred it if he had stayed away until she had gotten to the point she could understand her own emotional state. She cursed at her thoughts as he leaned closer and smiled into her eyes.

"You look tired," he informed her.

"I'm just coming back from work. It's been a long day," she offered as an explanation, her brain scrambled.

He leaned back with a wistful smile.

"Ah, yes. You got a job at a shelter here."

He traced a finger across her cheekbones. She leaned into his hand as he looked over her face, concerned. Knowing he was worried about her comforted her so she said, "I'm just exhausted; nothing a good night's sleep will not cure." He hadn't changed; his love was still readily available to her. Too bad she couldn't say the same about herself.

"You need a few days off. I know that you love your job, but you're not looking so good, angel." His voice was soothing, but they'd had this debate many times and she wasn't about to do it again.

"Let's save this discussion for later," Kalilah said, then stood up and reached for her sister's mug. Jonathan stood too, intercepted her hand and pulled her to him with it. He smothered her in his signature embrace and lowered one hand to her chin to tilt her face up to his.

"You're not mad at me, are you? I don't want to fight; I just missed you so much and I just wanted to see you." He looked at her intently.

She leaned closer and rewarded him with a small kiss.

"I know you worry about me, but I promise you that I'm taking care of myself." She moved out of his embrace and beckoned Kaiya closer. "I guess you've met my sister?"

"Yes, she definitely kept me entertained while waiting for you."

"I aim to entertain, especially when guests are worried," said Kaiya.

He squeezed Kalilah's hands, gave a reassuring brush of his lips against her skin before he released her. She immediately felt bereft as he directed a shy smile at Kaiya.

"I can't say for sure that I'm still not worried."

Since he was here now, she felt the tiredness slipping away, like it was a heavy blanket that was being towed away. The evening that had seemed so stifling was suddenly beautiful; the sun was streaming in through the window. The sound of traffic came in a muted roar and she felt compelled to show him around Montréal.

"We're going out!"

"We are?" Jonathan looked at her in surprise, and even Kaiya looked at her askance. "You should rest."

Her smile widened at his concern.

"I'm suddenly not as tired as I originally thought. I want to show you all of my favorite places in the city. Let me go freshen up!"

She went towards her bedroom, and Kaiya followed her.

"What's going on with you?"

"I'm just happy," she answered simply.

"I can see that, but what about Finn?"

"What about him?" The one word robbed her of her former enthusiasm; she stopped her contemplation of her wardrobe. She returned to the bed with a cotton blouse in her hand. "In fact, I don't want to talk about it."

Kaiya walked closer to engulf her sister in a hug.

"I understand. Enjoy your night."

Enjoy it they did. Her lost enthusiasm returned and, when they hit the streets, the joy was almost manic. She had dragged him to the old port for dinner and then they strolled through Saint Catherine Street as well as the underground city. They walked around until she began to feel the effects of her sudden effervescence. The tiredness slipped up on her as suddenly as it had left. She couldn't hide it from him and when he suggested that they return home, she was relieved.

When they reached the door, Jonathan stopped Kalilah from opening the door to her condo.

"I want some time alone with you before we go in."

"Oh."

He took advantage of her surprise and tugged her into his arms; she looked up at him. He looked so happy. It was difficult to keep eye contact with him. She feared what he may see in her eyes.

"I love you," he said suddenly.

"I know you do," she responded, and brushed her lips to his. He kissed her then – a slow tangle of tongues. She finally pulled away from the kiss, feeling guilty. Who was being unfaithful to whom in this situation?

Sleeping arrangements had been surprisingly easy to manage, with Jonathan opting to take the couch. Kalilah tossed and turned all night. She spent the bulk of the night paying court to doubts that had her fretting until the blush of dawn hit the sky. Even if she had been happy to reconnect with Jon, she spent the night in quiet contemplation of her future. Somehow, she had lost sight of the reason she had returned home, and that thought was disturbing.

When day broke completely, Kalilah got out of bed with her head and her heart still in a jumble. She was determined to make the best of the day, though.

"You're up early," said Jon as she stepped into the kitchen. She treated herself to a long look at his face, drinking in the love that shone in his eyes.

"Good morning to you as well." She smiled back at him. Kalilah heard the doorbell ring and the patter of her sister's feet as she went to answer it.

Jonathan moved to kiss her, and she sidled into the embrace. His mouth covered hers and his tongue probed her mouth. She was only too eager to duel with him, matching every movement with a couple of well-timed bites. Her hands had wound around his neck without her being aware that she moved, and he held her in a firm embrace with her face tilted up, a move that robbed her of ease of movement. She gave as good as she got, trying desperately to feel the sensations that she felt in Finn's kisses. She never felt them. Jon's kisses didn't give her those butterflies.

She finally pulled away from him to catch her breath. He leaned into their embrace and she pressed further into his body still searching for a spark of those tingly sensations she felt with Finn. She felt the proof of his passion and immediately became embarrassed by the bulge between them. Jonathan smiled down at her with an almost apologetic look.

The next sound that came was growl, and it shattered the air around them. It came from behind them and it startled them both. Jonathan and Kalilah jumped apart, and she whirled to find Finn regarding the two of them with fury in his eyes.

Kalilah stumbled backward, farther from Jonathan. Shame and disgust fought a tug-of-war in her stomach. She shifted to the side and tried to make introductions.

"Finn this is…"

"Jonathan Sawyer," he completed without inflection.

"Finn Tremblay."

"You're Kalilah's ex-husband," Jonathan offered. She wondered if she'd ever told Jon Finn's last name.

"Is that so," Finn turned his attention to Kalilah but only for a second.

Kalilah couldn't help but feel as if the universe was against her. Her sister looked amused at the entire situation.

"Jonathan decided to surprise me with a visit," Kalilah said in response. Why was she even explaining herself to him?

"I see. Well, I was hoping for your companionship at breakfast."

"And why would you hope that?" Jonathan asked.

The room was silent for a full second, and Kaiya moved away from Finn and closer to her sister. Kalilah saw it as a show of solidarity, and she was thankful to have her sister here.

She resolutely faced Finn and grabbed hold of Jonathan's hand; a move Finn didn't miss if the tightening of his jaw was a sign to go by.

"I'm sorry Finn but I can't have breakfast with you this morning."

"She has plans with me already," Jon said.

"I believe Mrs. Tremblay can speak for herself."

"You both need to stop it now!"

Finn continued to ignore her. Taking hold of Jonathan's hand earlier showed where her loyalty lay.

"Seems you're a bit thick," Jonathan ventured.

***

"You're the one foolish enough to come here and kiss another man's wife. Maybe you should return to Seattle like a good little boy and wait until she calls." Finn wouldn't let this piece of shit come here and try to destroy all he had built – and was still trying to build – with his wife. He wouldn't back down for anyone who threatened his marriage.

Jonathan boldly took a step forward until he was in Finn's personal space with a scowl like thunder on his face.

"I think you're the one interrupting, and you need to leave right now!"

Finn had half a mind to punch this asshole in the face for touching his wife and then entering his personal space. The two men stood toe to toe, but the only similarity was their height. They were as different as night and day. Finn was white with a lean, muscular build with dark hair, while Jonathan was bulkier with blond hair. Jonathan was bald with a beard, while Finn's face was cleanly shaven. Finn also realized that Jonathan talked a lot. He was all noise and no action. Finn's quiet presence was more dominating. Finn didn't view this chatterbox as a threat at all.

"I'll leave as soon as you tell Kalilah the truth."

He fumbled, shifted somewhat, and took a small step backwards.

"I have no idea what you mean, you wretched bastard. I do know you're jealous you couldn't make her happy and now you don't want her to be happy with me."

"Oh, I think I've been making her very happy," Finn replied with rising amusement.

"Yeah, like she'll ever be happy with husband that wasn't going to marry her if there was no company to sweeten the deal."

Finn kept a straight face; both he and Lilah knew the truth of what happened five years ago.

Jonathan pressed on with a wide smile.

"You see, I know all about how you tried to use her and now she's happy with someone else and it just eats you up doesn't it?"

"You bet it does. Now please explain to her why you've been in Montréal these past two months and you're only now showing up on her doorstep." Kalilah turned to look at Jonathan this time and caught the brief flicker in his eyes.

"Jonathan, is that true?"

"All things are uncertainties when evidence is not presented." Finn said. "As much as I'd like to stay here and listen to you try to wiggle your way out of answering, I can't. I'm a busy man with a company that needs managing." He turned away from them, and with one last glance directed at Kalilah, and a nod at Kaiya, he headed for the door.

"Think I'll leave as well. Give you two some privacy." Kaiya left.

Kalilah disentangled her hand from Jonathan's and moved to the couch.

"The son of a bitch has balls, waltzing in here like he owned the place. "

"I asked you a question. How long have you been in the country?"

"Why was he even here, Kalilah?" he asked, his voice filled with anger. He was deliberately avoiding her question.

She ignored his question and asked him again if what Finn said was true. Jonathan paused his rant.

"Of course it isn't true. I drove into the city last night. It took me almost two days drive to get up here."

"So why would Finn say that then?"

"Angel, it's obvious that he doesn't want to lose you, so he'll say anything to hurt us."

She mulled over what he said and decided to accept it for now. However, in her mind, something still wasn't right. She didn't think Finn would ever lie to her, but then again Jon had never lied to her either.

CHAPTER 13

THE NEXT MORNING AS KALILAH PREPARED FOR WORK, she heard a knock on her door and opened it to find Kaiya waiting. She waved her in before returning to her wardrobe. Last night had been difficult. After her discussion with Jon, she'd come to bed and thought over everything that had happened that day. She could still see the look on Finn's face when she'd taken Jon's hand.

"How are you feeling this morning?"

"Like I'm stuck between a rock and a hard place."

Kaiya quirked her eyebrows at that.

"You do know that you don't have to choose either of them right. You and I can stay here and be hot single girls for the rest of our lives." Her sister began to twerk and she couldn't help but smile.

"You are so silly. I spoke to Jonathan about the things that Finn said and he denied it."

"Did you ask him to see his ticket?"

"No, he said he drove into the country."

"What about his passport? It should have the border entry stamp?"

"I thought of that, but I didn't want it to seem like I didn't trust him?"

Kaiya snorted at her words.

"Still hiding your head in the sand?"

The bitter accusation drew bitter bile to her throat and annoyed her completely. The calm she had maintained all morning broke, and she erupted.

"Do you think this is easy for me?"

"Look, Kalilah..." Kaiya started to say but she was past being talked down to by people around her.

"No, you look, you're always here with sage advice and I just want you to stop. I am not in the headspace to receive any judgement right now. I know that everything that has happened is my own fault. I don't need you to remind me of that fact," she pressed on with uncharacteristic vehemence.

"I wasn't trying to judge you," Kaiya tried to mollify her, "and I'm sorry you feel that way. I just want you to be happy because I know how you're probably feeling right now. I was in love once. Well at least I thought I was. We were young, I was barely out of secondary school."

Her anger drained away in the face of her sister's sudden candor.

"I'm sorry, I didn't know."

"You couldn't possibly have known. By the time we met, you'd already left."

The elephant in the room she was hoping to ignore but couldn't. Kalilah sighed.

"I'm sorry I wasn't here for you."

"No need to apologize, I understand why you needed to leave."

"It still doesn't make me feel any less guilty about leaving you behind. Come lay on my bed."

After her sister laid down, she laid down next to her. Kalilah pressed on, "Tell me about this man who stole my little sister's heart."

Her sister was quiet for a little bit.

"It's a long story. Are you sure you want to hear it since you have your own life to figure out?"

"I'm fine. I need the distraction."

"His name was Tyler Landry and I met him four years ago. We met at one of those house parties I was always sneaking off to with Jalissa. Anyway, six months after we began dating, I found out I was pregnant…" Her sister's voice faltered, but Kalilah remained silent.

By the time Kaiya was done with the tale, both sisters' eyes were brimming with tears. She couldn't believe everything her sister just told her. Her heart truly went out to her. She felt the guilt rising again. She should have been there when Kaiya needed her most. She knew then that she would never leave her behind again.

"I am so sorry that you lost your son. I'm sorry for everything else that you lost." Kalilah wrapped her arms around her sister's body as her own sobs threatened to overpower the little control she had left. This explained her sister's behavior when they were in stores selling baby clothes. Her sister was still grieving.

"Me too," her sister said weakly. "I wish I got a chance to tell him goodbye and how much I loved and wanted him."

"Maybe you still can. We can go to the lake and light candles in his honor and say a prayer for him. You can also tell him how much you love him. Although I am sure he knows." After everything Kaiya told her, Kalilah knew that she needed to sort through this triangle. Life was too short.

"I love that idea. Thank you Lah."

"What about Tyler? Have you seen or heard from him since?"

"No, and I don't care to. I loved him but he didn't love me in return. Father was right about him after all." Kaiya's words hanged in the air between the sisters. Kalilah doubted that her father was right about anything concerning his daughters' lives, a fact she wouldn't bring up to Kaiya.

Not when her emotions were still so raw.

The comfortable silence lengthened between them until Kalilah confessed, "I'm scared," and it was Kaiya's turn to wrap her in her arms. The admission took a lot out of her and she couldn't hold on to the ruse that she was in control; she could no longer maintain the illusion that she had any idea of how her life was turning out to be. Everything was rapidly going out of her hands and in a direction she hadn't planned. She knew she needed to talk to Finn as soon as possible. First though, she needed to get ready for work.

***

"Bad day?" a cheerful voice called in front of her.

The muscles of her neck protested at the sharp movement as her head jolted upward into the face of one of the Case Coordinators – Raleigh – standing in front of her. Raleigh had been the one to interview her for the position. She was a black woman, probably in her mid-forties, who had wasted no time in offering her the job position while explaining the challenges of the shelter.

Since they were the only two black women working there with Caribbean roots, they instantly became friends. Kalilah took a close look at Raleigh and saw she was slightly bent over and looked pale. She had lost her husband to colon cancer, and ever since his death, she had dedicated her life to giving back to others.

"Just catching my breath."

"Honey, I've worked here since forever and I've given up on catching my breath," she returned with a cheeky smile.

"That's encouraging."

"You'll get used to it."

Kalilah looked around the kitchen, with its set of neat but old mismatched chairs. Her eyes closed and she pictured the kind of clientele it catered to.

"We'll see. I love what I do here and wouldn't trade it for anything."

"That's the spirit. It takes a lot out of you but in the end it's totally worth it," Raleigh offered.

"You're right."

Raleigh smiled heavily at that.

"At least, that's what my mother tells me every time I call her to rant about my lack of a social life."

" Who needs clubs?" Kalilah quipped with one raised eyebrow and they both chuckled.

The rest of the day passed quickly, and Kalilah was anxious to see Finn later. She had a lot to discuss with him.

***

"A Miss Kalilah Anderson to see you," the disembodied voice informed him through the phone.

The words had him spilling his drink in surprise. Then the panic descended. Was something wrong? Something had gone wrong, that was the only reason he could think to have Kalilah at his door, but for the life of him he couldn't think of any scenario.

"Sir? Is everything alright? Do I tell her you are not currently at home?"

Finn answered simply.

"Send the lady up; always send her up." He then hung up while eyeing the phone in trepidation. The moments passed and his panic gave way to fear as the doubts started to creep in. She probably came to politely tell him she was returning to Seattle with Jonathan. He didn't know what he would do if she decided to leave.

You're losing her, said the insidious whisper in his head, and Finn scowled at the unwelcome intrusion.

"No, I can't, we love each other."

You love her, but she loves him, the voice replied and Finn bit back a curse. When he walked in on them embracing, it had taken all his will not to tear the man apart. What right did he have laying his dirty fingers on his woman?

She had made her decision very clear when she had taken hold of Jonathan's hand and allowed him to stay at her place, even after Finn told her the truth about the man. He probably shouldn't have called him out like that, but the emotions riding him were too strong for his control at that moment. His love for her was so deep that the thought of being away from her a second time didn't sit well with his heart, soul, or body. All he wanted was to settle down in his marital life.

Of course, the protective surges he had towards her were working overtime when he had seen the smug leer that man directed at Kalilah when she had turned her back. He had lost his mind by flinging those facts around in a confrontation that had changed nothing.

Finn knocked back the cognac in one quick swallow and contemplated another drink. No, he would need a clear head.

Maybe he needed to face it and move on; chemistry was not enough for a marriage. If that were the case, Kalilah wouldn't have left him in the first place. His thoughts did not sit well with him, and it had him pacing from one edge of the room to another.

The sound of his door buzzing saved him from the scenes in his mind, every image more of a torment than the last.

"Come on in." He beckoned and she stepped through the door.

Kalilah moved into the room and quickly glanced around. The decor was masculine, heavy, but the pieces of furniture were modern except for the stuffed cushion that faced the curtains. She had an idea what he needed it for. Finn was always drawn to views and she knew his tendencies to do his best thinking looking over scenery. No reason not to do that from the comfort of the overstuffed and large monstrosity that sat squat in front of the balcony windows.

Kalilah turned at the voice. She realized she hadn't heard him in the middle of her rambling thoughts.

"I'm sorry, did you say something?" she asked sheepishly.

"Want something to drink?" The innocent enquiry made her stomach clench nervously. The cup of coffee she had drank at work rolled in her stomach.

"No, I'm good," she replied before turning away from him.

"Would you like a tour of this place?"

He gave her an intense once-over, as if trying to decipher the many emotions she was sure showed on her face.

"Maybe another time. Can I sit?" she asked.

"Sure you can." He gestured to the sofa and she went to sit on it. "What brings you by?"

"I've been thinking a lot about my future and I remember you mentioning the building you recently acquired..." The words stuck in her throat, a throat that was as suddenly as dry as the Sahara.

"Kalilah, spit it out already." His words were sharp and impatient.

"Well, I've decided to go ahead and look into opening my own non-profit residence for women. I came here to talk about the building you mentioned. I want to know everything about it."

"That's wonderful news, Kalilah. Does that mean you plan on staying in the country indefinitely?"

She saw the hope in his eyes and hated that her next words would dampen it.

"I plan to stay until I get it off the ground. After that, I can always find someone to run things in my absence."

"Are you sure that this is what you want?"

"Finn, will you tell me about the building or not?"

***

Two hours later the table was littered with papers, discarded cups of coffee, and a cookie packet that had only crumbles left in it. Finn raised his head to catch the last rays of a dying sun and glanced at his watch to confirm.

"Is that the time?" Kalilah grabbed his hand and exclaimed.

"I can't believe it; I guess time flies when you're having fun."

"Fun indeed," she murmured, and reached down to grab her purse that was lying on the floor, "but I have to get home."

"Do you?" he asked as he ran his fingers over her shoulder and down her collar bone leaving a trail of heat in its wake.

"What are we doing?" she asked, her voice breathless from the havoc his fingers were causing.

"I've missed you so much, wife," his voice sounded breathless as well.

He pulled her closer, gently cradling her neck with his hand and he slipped his lips onto hers. He devoured her, as though this was their last night on Earth. Denied desires rode her with a vengeance, and she spiraled into the madness that drove moans out of her. She could taste a smoky spice on his tongue. *Brandy,* her mind supplied; she could get drunk on that taste alone. He scooped her up by her thighs and settled her atop his, before pressing his body against her and intensifying their kiss.

Finn broke the kiss and breathed heavily against her neck as he whispered, "You don't know what you do to me. You don't know how happy you have made me." He tried to kiss her again but Kalilah ducked her face.

If what she did to him was anything like she felt, then they were well and truly lost.

"Look at me." It was a command but more than the tone, his voice held promises and they weakened her. How could she even begin to resist the hold he had on her? But she did.

Kalilah tried to get off him and put some distance between them, but he held on to her.

"I didn't come here for this, Finn." He leaned towards her, and her body was shamelessly drawn to his.

"Why did you come then?" he challenged, confident of his victory. Confident in her responses, even if her lips said no, her body had melted under his hands.

"I came to..." Her voice was too breathy; she took a deep breath and tried again. "I came to discuss my residence."

"Something we could have done at my office," he returned with a smile that promised carnal things to come. Her body wanted everything in that smile. Her body clenched around nothing and she almost moaned out loud. She sucked in air as he stalked her with single-minded intensity. She couldn't even turn her eyes away from his, not when the look in his eyes resounded in her, when it brought her senses to life.

"Tell me why you came to my place, Lilah." The words were delivered in a husky voice that wrapped itself around her like a thick blanket, except it offered no comfort, only madness.

"Not for this," she breathed, trying to hide her face in case he could read the truth there.

"Liar!" he retorted and tilted her head up to face his.

Kalilah sighed as his warm lips returned, wreaking havoc on her senses. He moved to the long, slender column of her throat, nipped at her collarbones and kissed the hollow of her throat, before trailing his tongue along her skin in a lingering kiss. She wanted his lips on hers, his tongue dueling with hers, but he refused her. Tantalizing and torturing all at once, it proved too much for her body. She began to move her hips, which caused her to feel his erection. Her body hungered for more, much more. Kalilah swallowed the lump that threatened to cut off her breathing.

"Please," she moaned, and Finn groaned at the breathy, pleading voice. He was a sucker for her voice, and it was especially potent now that she was wild with desire. He covered her mouth with his and tasted her lips again and again. Coffee and her – a heady aphrodisiac.

Her hand curled around his neck as she leaned into his embrace. She wanted to feel him, her hands roamed his broad back and suddenly she was unwilling to have a piece of clothing holding her back from her prize.

"Please." She tugged at his shirt and Finn shrugged it off in one smooth move.

Her hands landed on his body and he shivered at the airy touch. She moved over him, her eyes trailing everywhere she touched. Lower, and lower still until she brushed his belt buckle.

Finn captured her hands and drew her into another kiss. She eased away and stroked lower, her fingers intent on discovery.

"Please."

Finn groaned, "Are you sure you want to? There won't be any erasing this, I won't conveniently forget it if you wake up with regrets tomorrow. I don't want you to regret this when you wake up tomorrow."

"I want you." She looked at him with such a hunger as she said those words, and he knew he would never be able to deny her; not this, not anything.

"Let's move this to our bed then," he ordered. *Our?* A raw urgency ripped through him as he then hauled her up fireman's style and raced into his bedroom. He paused at the foot of his bed and he placed her gently onto it.

The setting was suddenly intimate. He didn't have a shirt on. Kalilah bit her lips as she looked at the view. His broad chest had well-defined muscles, beaten to perfection by hours at the gym.

The muscles rippled, and when she tested their firmness, her fingers bounced.

She looked up to gauge his reaction to that. Finn wore a heated look that had her pulling her hand away.

"Don't you dare pull your hand away, touch me wherever you want to," he invited.

Emboldened, her fingers trailed every ridge until it led to the place it was barred from. She flicked her hand against the dusty trail of hair and enjoyed the way he held himself in place, as if one movement was going to cost him dearly.

Finn swept her hands away when he could no longer stand the teasing fingers. He tugged at her blouse and helped her discard her clothing, piece by piece, until they were scattered around the room. He then indulged his every fantasy. He looked over her with such intensity and for so long that she lifted her hands to hide, becoming self-conscious.

"Please don't, I want to see you. I've had dreams of this moment for so long. Far too long." With those words barely past his lips, he ravished her. She barely had a second to breathe before his lips covered hers and turned her into something wild. Even in her surprise, she didn't stop the kiss;

she rode it as Finn plundered her mouth. Strong arms pulled her closer, and he settled between her thighs. She wrapped her legs around waist and pressed her core into his groin, and moaned into his mouth when she felt his erection. His hands roamed until they tangled in her hair; his grip tightened almost to the point of pain but she rode on the waves of so much pleasure that the discomfort paled in comparison.

She arched up to him, pressing herself against him, hoping to alleviate some of the need that was building up.

Finn tore his mouth away and gasped as she continued to writhe against him; even through his clothing he felt her heat. But he pulled away. He had to visit her breasts; pert, beautiful, and poking insistently into his chest. He flicked a nipple with the flat tip of his tongue, and she moaned. A feverish sound that filled the room.

"So responsive." His husky voice grated on her senses. His finger drew concentric circles that got closer and closer to that spot but not quite. "I wonder what happens when I do this," he mused then bent and sucked her most sensitive nub.

Kalilah almost arched off the bed, her body buffeted by a hunger she was only beginning to learn the depths of. His roaming hand reached the junction between her thighs and she held her breath – wondering, waiting.

He made her wait for it. One beat, two heartbeats later, he delved in. Her heightened anticipation was her undoing.

His fingers had barely brushed her secret place when a hot warmth mingled with a drunken daze, sweeping her from the very top of her head to the tips of her toes, clouding her vision. Her body vibrated and her voice, it was stolen from her or she would have screamed.

Kalilah panted through the onslaught.

"I need more!" She still had an ache that had become even more urgent.

Finn held her as she lost her senses, enjoying the way her legs had tightened around his hips, the way her body had arched, the dusky smooth expanse of skin that demanded kisses and worship.

She came back down to Earth, and he was pleased that she still wanted more, that she still wanted him. Her hands delved lower and tugged at his belt, and this time he didn't tell her no. He left the bed briefly to dispose of the troublesome clothing and returned, his warm flesh rubbing against hers.

His body surrounded her, and when he reached between her thighs, Kalilah parted her legs in acquiescence and he crawled between them.

She followed the trail of her fingers and delved even lower until she got a good look at his member and swallowed. She wondered how it would fit inside her tiny body.

"Second thoughts?" She looked up to catch his worried gaze.

"No," she answered with certainty.

"Good." There was no more room for further words. He leaned forward to capture her lips with his. His fingers returned to tracing her wet slit, with the occasional bump against her clit.

He removed his moist fingers from her body, positioned his manhood at her opening, and plunged in. The pain from that intrusion was instantaneous. It was more than a sting. It was more like pulling of a bandage dressing but much more visceral, much deeper.

She yelped. The feeling of having him inside of her was foreign.

All movement stalled and she knew her secret was no longer one.

"Kalilah, you're still..."

"Yes," she breathed. What kind of loser still had their virginity at twenty-five? She wanted to hide from the sheer embarrassment of it all, but she wanted him so badly. Her desire overpowered her humiliation.

"We can't do this." He tried to pull away, but she tightened her legs around him, trapping him between her thighs. Her hand trailing down to what she wanted – and by God she was going to have it. All of it.

"Please, Finn, I'm sure. Don't make me wait any longer." She didn't want to beg, but she would if she had to.

He needed no further encouragement, he relented and entered her again slowly, giving her time to adjust this time. He held his breath, his control impeccable, and her eyes were focused on his, reading every naked emotion as if he was an open book. He didn't give her much time to settle before he was sliding out of her and then back in. The pain she'd felt earlier was replaced by unbridled pleasure. She moaned. A long breath, which threatened to empty her of oxygen and thoughts, escaped her lips with each stroke, barely allowing her to relax and luxuriate in each new pleasure.

Wave after wave until she was pushing against him, hungering for that long glide of smooth flesh and the coming pleasure that threatened to undo her.

Her body clenched and then released him in a warm, wet hold of tight muscle; he was losing control fast, too fast.

It hit her with the force of a speeding train, her body arched involuntarily as she screamed his name.

He had only one glance to appreciate the picture she made, eyes wild, body arched, eyes glazed with desire, legs tight and nails dug deep into his back. He did not feel it; he only felt the heat of her wet warmth squeezing him. Two more thrusts, and he descended into blackness, calling her name.

***

Sometime in the night he woke up to a warm body tangled around him. The reality of her in his bed felt unreal.

But it felt right. She peeled back his control with practiced ease and without so much a word – she had only to be there.

"What are you thinking about?"

The words startled him, as he had thought she was fast asleep.

"Why do you think I'm thinking about anything?"

"You're being very quiet."

"I was thinking about you." He answered easily, but there was no way he was going to tell her exactly what he was thinking without sounding convoluted and confused.

Her body leaned into him more as her head blindly searched for a more comfortable position on his arm, before settling back onto his skin. The warmth of her body soothed something in him, the way she curled against him solved hurts he didn't know he carried in him; her mere presence quenched an ache he had accepted as normal for too long. His only problem was that it was morning, and daylight was not kind to doubts.

He just wanted to enjoy the feel of her nestled closely against him, her warm flesh on his. The emotions in his chest tried to overwhelm him again with their intensity. That was one part of him – the other part was more uncivilized, and he wondered if this was how people with personality disorders felt. *Torn in various directions?* Because there was a part of him that wanted nothing better than to shout out loud. He wanted to take an ad out in the paper, or maybe even climb to the rooftop and shout until the whole city heard him. Never in all his dreams and imagination did he believe that she was still going to be a virgin.

When he plunged through her hymen he had blanked out with shock and joy battling fiercely for dominance, while dread closely followed. Dread had won out and he had faltered at the enormous gift she was giving him, he had tried to do the right thing, tried to be a better man and a better man would not be selfish. His body had rebelled at it, his erection throbbing against her opening fiercely. The desire riding him until he was sure his skin was vibrating but he had wrenched control from the madness in his veins and moved back but she was having none of that. Her legs had tightened around him, her eyes flashing with determination and desire, she had taken what she wanted from him and—*fuck!* That was hot, he couldn't even dream of saying no again.

For the longest while, he had thought she stepped out on their vows. Many times, he had conjured the phantom face of her many lovers. The presence of the guy at her place yesterday was a direct blow to his ego. His vision had swum with a red tinge and he had wanted nothing better than to pound him into the ground.

He'd baited him too, waiting for a chance to wipe the smug look off his face, but even if the guy didn't have a lot of sense, he had a good deal of self-preservation instinct, the bastard. To walk in the door and find his woman in another man's embrace was a test many men would have failed. The violence the scene awoke in him had staggered him. Staying there and not killing the smug bastard was a test of patience and control he never wanted to face again.

She stretched in the bed, and her hand got so close to discovering the semi-erection he was sporting, ably turning his thoughts from bloody murder to desire, not quite a semi anymore but it wasn't going to get any action, not this morning.

His erection twitched as he tried to battle his rising desires. Her hand continued its lazy glide on his abdomen, tracing his skin with faint strokes and occasional edge of her nails. He captured it and was rewarded with a low laugh. The minx knew what she was doing too, fuck any illusions of control he thought he had. He had taken her two times already last night in a frenzy of wild desire riding them both, as if making up for lost time. He was about to take her again for the third time.

CHAPTER 14

"GOOD MORNING," KALILAH CALLED AS SHE DISENTANGLED her body from his and made for the edge of the bed. Her intentions were obvious, but tell that to the monster perking up at his groin area.

The morning light did her full justice. Glittering caramel skin and legs that went forever, symmetrical features with long limbs and mouth-watering curves; curly hair which created interesting shadows that hid and showed certain things. His manhood was throbbing now at the sight.

He murmured when he could find his voice. A low, out of breath, husky tone.

"Morning, beautiful." Kalilah paused in the act of climbing out of bed to look back at him. He looked at her with a mix of hunger and satisfaction, bringing a faint blush to her face.

"I have to go," she said in haste, and his heart crumbled.

"Why don't you stay for breakfast. I could prepare eggs?"

"I don't want to... I mean, I don't want you to think it's..." she said and his heart sank even more.

"What don't you want me to think?" his words curt.

"That what happened last night changes anything," she finished in a rush.

"On the contrary, it changes everything," his voice was deliberately low.

"Don't be difficult now, Finn," she replied.

"Are you on any form of birth control?" Her eyes widened and her mouth turned agape. "I'm guessing by your facial expression that you're not, and considering we didn't use protection last night... we have much to discuss."

"I think we're safe from any unwanted pregnancies." Her voice faltered. "Right now, I really need to get home since I have a guest that is probably worried sick about me."

Unwanted? He got out of bed in one quick move and she shifted out of the way quickly. He stood in front of her, unashamed, and took his own sweet time tugging his trousers on and stalked out of the room. When he returned to the room she was fully dressed. He handed her an envelope.

"Open it," he encouraged. He was playing dirty but he didn't want to lose his wife. She needed a nudge and he didn't mind being the one to give it. He saw the curiosity in her eyes when she opened the envelope. Pictures, dozens of them with only one subject; Jonathan.

"What's this?"

"Look at the dates." he prompted.

"That's the date I arrived in Montréal," she replied, something seeming to elude her, a niggling thought.

"Recognize any landmarks?" he prompted again. "I don't know what his deal is, but he has been lying to you."

She took another look at the pictures and she headed for the door.

"Lilah, wait, don't go like this. Let me take you home."

"Owen is waiting downstairs," she returned evenly, and exited his apartment with the Polaroids clutched in hand.

***

Of course, she had heard about the classic 'walk of shame' but she never thought she'd ever have to do that walk. Trust fate to give her a completely new twist on the whole thing. Try 'walk of shame, anger, and doubt, with a pinch of self-loathing.' These were all the emotions going through her now.

Kalilah punched the elevator button with more force than necessary, and ignored the other occupants. She did not want to face the sharply-dressed morning crowd and the knowing looks that scanned her and found her wanting. She had enough in her head without the judgment they were itching to deliver.

When her floor number lit up, she slid through the aromatic crush of bodies and out of the car. The hallways were quiet enough that her own footsteps echoed hollowly, but even the setting had no impact on her.

The doorknob turned effortlessly in her hand as she pushed it. The apartment was quiet. Kalilah idly wondered if anyone was home, even as the small twinge of guilt wiggled within her when she remembered how she had spent the night out without telling anyone else where she was.

However, she didn't regret spending the night with Finn. He'd brought her so much pleasure.

"Enjoyed your night?" Jonathan's sarcastic words jolted her out of her thoughts. She had hoped for some time to... what? Shower? Think? Frame her accusations properly?

"I did actually," she agreed.

"I can see that," the words were perfectly neutral again and she dared to look at him this time.

He looked angry as he looked her over.

"Did you spend the night with him?" Kalilah winced at accusation in his voice. She took a seat away from him. She didn't need to ask him who he was talking about. She knew and she had no intentions of lying to him.

She admitted to him about spending the night at Finn's and she could see the hurt in his eyes.

She apologized profusely for hurting him. However, she didn't apologize for doing what she had done with Finn. It would have been a lie.

"How could you do this to us? I thought we loved each other?"

She refused to be the only one who was placed on 'trial'. She fished the Polaroids out of her handbag, placed them on the table between them without a single comment, and waited for his reaction.

He picked up the first one in a lazy move and sat bolt upright the next second. Within minutes he had riffled through the small stack and arranged them back meticulously face down on the space between the two of them without commenting.

"Is there anything you need to tell me?" How she got the words out of her heavy throat would always be a mystery to her. "I want to know why you've been in Montréal for the past two months, and why you showed up to my home only three days ago. Come to think about it, I never gave you my address, how did you know where to find me?"

He turned around and waved her claims away.

"That's preposterous! How on Earth are you even buying into this nonsense? I mean, isn't this the work of your jealous, bitter, soon to be ex-husband trying every means possible to tear us apart?"

"This has nothing to do with my husband. I am more concerned that you lied to me. Why are you still lying to me, and why are you still avoiding my questions?"

"So now he's your husband?"

Jonathan stood up and walked away from the table, away from the incriminating pictures and accusations. He glanced at every part of the room except where she was seated.

"I knew about you for a very long time before we met personally."

She was stunned by his admission, and listened as he continued his story.

"Your father came down to my newly-opened private investigation business in Seattle. I must admit that I was impressed. I was barely out of school and barely established. The idea of work was pointed toward survival when he told me he wanted me to keep a close eye on his daughter.

A rich young girl in the big bad city, clearly enjoying her first taste of freedom could run into a few problems. I jumped at the opportunity. You were the only client I had for the past five years. Your father's monthly payments kept me housed, dressed and fed. I never needed another client."

"Is that why your apartment was right in front of mine?" Kalilah listened with a heart that threatened to bleed out, but she did not look at him anymore.

"Yes. Your father wanted me to shadow you and report everything back to him. Watching you day in and day out, I fell in love with your gentle spirit and kind nature. I knew I needed to meet you, so on that day you needed help with your groceries I decided to finally make your acquaintance." Everything he was saying made sense. It broke her heart to find out that her life was still a script written by people who had no business interfering in other people's lives.

His words hurt, but she refused to acknowledge the pain, at least not yet.

"I was a job to you? Did my father give you a bonus for dating me too? A good plan to keep other men away?"

"It was nothing like that, angel, I swear it. Your father didn't find out about our relationship until you came back. He told me to stay away from you, but I couldn't. You have to know that what I feel. What we have together is real." He took a step toward her, but the look on her face must have halted his steps since he stopped.

"Real? You tell me that I was a job paid for by my father, and you expect me to believe that you love me? Our entire relationship was built on lies!" She returned as she shook her head.

"I'm sorry, angel. I swear, I love you, and we can work through this. I know we can. Think about us and our future. We're so close."

"There is no us. Not anymore." Her heart was breaking. He was a huge part of her life for almost two years – one year as friends and nine months as a couple – and it hurt to know that she was only a job to him.

"It him isn't it? That ex-husband of yours." He looked straight at her with eyes that were red-rimmed and glistening with tears.

"This isn't about him. He didn't make you take the job from my father or lie to me," she returned.

"Please, Kalilah. Believe me, I never meant to hurt you. Listen, we've both hurt each other. We're even. Please, angel." He took a step towards her, and she was slow to react when he took her hand in his and knelt before her. "We can work this out."

"No, we can't. Goodbye, Jonathan. Go back to wherever you've been these last few months."

"Damn, I don't think I ever had a chance," he lamented.

She turned her head away from him, and the truth hit her as he gathered his belongings and left.

Kalilah hopped in the shower and cried her eyes out. When she was done crying, she got out of the shower and dressed. There were things to be done, things she needed to take care of before she lost the anger coursing through her.

Her parents' mansion was oddly quiet. Kalilah did not hear any of the many workers that frequented her family's home. Bates waved her into the home, and she asked him if her father was in at the moment. This scene seemed like déjà vu.

Standing at the threshold she took a deep breath as she tried to shore up her defenses; Richard was not capable of emotionally hurting her again, though try he would. She needed her defenses for the little girl who still yearned for her parents' approval. The door to her father's office swung open before she had a chance to knock. The open door revealed a very irate Finn.

"Lilah?"

"Finn?"

"I wasn't expecting to see you here."

"Yeah well, I wasn't expecting to be here today either." She stepped into the study. "Father."

"That simpleton told you, didn't he?" her father sighed, a bit of guilt in his words.

"You cannot change, can you? You cannot help yourself from playing God in other peoples' lives!" she yelled. Kalilah waited for some kind of response from the man but he simply snorted, turned his back to her and began to walk away.

"Typical of you!' she cried aloud. "Always the coward!"

He suddenly stopped walking and Kalilah knew she had struck a nerve. She had never spoken to her father in such hostile tone. She wasn't ever permitted to utter her grievances in such a disrespectful manner either. Everything was swept under the rug, and she was sick and tired of it.

Kalilah's father turned around to look at her.

"I will let those first few insolent words from your mouth slide, child!" He then turned from his daughter to look at the man standing beside her. "Talk to your wife. Make her see reason, son."

"I happen to enjoy seeing my wife all fired up," Finn said, then shrugged.

"Do you seriously think I would be okay with you having me followed? What's worse is that the person you paid to follow me around got personal... Too personal!"

"I want the best for my children. Have you any idea how easily you people of this new generation toss away real opportunities for fickle dreams that will never amount to anything?"

The words inflamed her because it was offensive to all her hard work.

"You did this for yourself, and your insane need to control everything. First you threatened me when I told you that I didn't want to marry Finn, and practically forced me to the altar. Adding Jonathan to the mix was a nice touch. Paying him to watch me? Whose idea was it for him to seduce me?"

"What? What are you talking about? How did he threaten you?" Finn asked.

Kalilah took on the task of explaining to Finn everything that happened that afternoon five years ago when her father had threatened to disown her if she didn't go through with the wedding.

She could see his face hardening at everything she was saying.

"You never told me any of this, Kalilah," Finn swore. "Richard what have you done? You blackmailed her into marrying me?!" His disgust colored the already tense atmosphere.

Her father bristled.

"Hold your tongue, girl; that business has been the Anderson family business and I will not stand to see the good family name go to ruin because I have the misfortune of birthing rebellious children."

"I'm rebellious because I refuse to let you control the direction of my life!" Her voice was pitched at a conversational level, but the words were iron, and directed at the man who had given her life.

A sneer blossomed on his face as he gave her his full attention.

"I'm sure it's been a real hardship having access to all the Anderson family funds," he replied sarcastically.

"It has been actually, living up to your expectations, but no more. I am done."

"Was I supposed to let you roam free and allow a slick-talker get his claws into our money?"

Richard admitted easily.

"You don't need to worry about gold-digging men, Father; you are the biggest one of them all," she replied.

"Mind your tongue before I take care of it, and you, permanently," he returned hotly.

"You won't lay a finger on her," Finn said calmly.

Richard continued imperiously.

"Everyone falls in line Kalilah, even you. You know what happens when you don't."

"You'll take away my credit cards? You can keep them!" Years of pain, disgust, and fears colored her words pitch black. "It all boils down to power, and you no longer have power over me. You can keep your money!"

"Walk out of here and you'll never see a single penny of mine again. What is he going to feed you on then? The salary he makes as a private dick chasing people for pennies?"

"I'm washing my hands of the lot of you." She was so tired now, and she couldn't care less about his opinions.

"You don't know what you are saying."

"Oh, yes I do, Father. I've never seen more clearly in my life. Threats will not hold me to this family any longer. I'm no longer that girl who would easily cower at bullies." The words came softly as she looked at her father losing his calm while she regained hers.

"Get out!"

"Richard, how can you do that to your own daughter?" Finn interrupted.

Kalilah looked at him. *Who was this blonde, blue-eyed man, standing up to her father for her?*

No one had ever tried to face Richard Anderson for her sake, not even her mother.

"She is no daughter of mine," Richard insisted with a hard look at Kalilah.

"Then I quit!" he returned.

"What?" Two voices in unison questioned his declaration. Kalilah looked at him with something close to awe.

"The company, you can keep it. I no longer have any interest in it." With that bombshell, Finn exited the study.

Kalilah exited hot on his heels and barely caught him at the door.

"You can't do that!"

"I can, and I have," he answered easily.

"You don't understand," she started to explain but he cut her off as he suddenly stopped walking and turned to face her, his face a mask of stubbornness, his jaw clenched. The blonde scruff on his face gave him a very wild look.

"Actually, for the very first time I do, the picture became clearer with that scene in there and I just want to say that if this is what you've been going through all these years, I am sorry for your pain and the part I've played in it."

Kalilah swallowed at his intensity.

"No, you don't need to apologize to me; I may have been hurt but then so were you. He used us. We were nothing but pawns to ensure the continuity of the business."

"I'm just glad it's all over now; he can keep his money and his company," he replied, eyes fixed on some distant sight.

"You can't quit. It's your dream and you've done such a good job with the company, don't stop now. You have so much more to do," she pleaded.

"I can't, knowing that he threatened you and cut you out of the family," he returned, his blue eyes searching hers.

"I don't think I've ever said it, but I am really proud of you. There are people whose livelihoods depend on you. It's bigger than me and you and all our sacrifices." She moved closer to him and placed her hand on his chest.

"The sacrifice was too great. Our entire marriage..." his pained voice trailed off.

"I know."

He turned away from her to look at the garden and said, "I'll rescind my resignation, but only because you asked me to. I'll let him stew for two weeks though."

"Make it a month." An impish suggestion that had him looking down at her. He brought his face down and leaned into her touch, lips tracing over her cheekbones before capturing her mouth in a hot kiss, his hand fisted in her hair.

CHAPTER 15

TWO WEEKS LATER, KALILAH LAY IN FINN'S BED, on her side, gazing out the window at the morning sunshine with a silly grin on her face. Memories of last night and the nights before coursed through her. She hadn't been to work in a fortnight. She was emotionally recovering from everything she learned, in addition to familiarizing herself to her husband's body. Jonathan kept calling and she kept sending him to voicemail. She planned on getting a local number anyway, since moving back to the States now seemed highly unlikely. Finn had kissed her into a frenzy when she had showed him the horrible texts Jon had sent her.

She and Finn spent the past two weeks in his condo doing nothing more than watching Netflix and making love.

They spoke of nothing of their future or their past. They simply basked in the passions of their present moment. Kaiya came over to Finn's once last week to sign some paperwork for her dance school, and Kalilah had told her sister everything that had transpired between her and their father. Her sister understood her need to distance herself. Kalilah still couldn't believe that she was here now. Laying in her husband's bed.

Last night had been a lot of things, all of them very good. The big hand splayed across her breasts shifted even lower, to her stomach, and her breathing hitched in anticipation of starting the day off the same way as they had left it last night. Her sore body warned against any rigorous action, but she woke up with a fine edge to her hunger and she would be ignoring anything that was not leading in the direction she wanted. She was introduced to multiple orgasms last night, and she couldn't wait to renew their acquaintance.

Finn shifted, pecked a good morning kiss on the back of her shoulder, and patted her bottom. Then the sleep-drugged touch became sharper, harder somehow.

Finally! That was the only thing she could think. He turned his lips towards hers, and his hands pulled her closer. Then his lips nudged hers open, and his tongue dipped into her mouth. She heard someone moan, and realized it was her. She did not want to be the only one moaning.

She lifted her hands and ran her fingers through his hair, running her nails along the skin at his neck and along his shoulders. It was his turn to moan. She would have smiled, but her mouth was busy.

She became aware of a hand on her leg, and she parted them for his insistent fingers. They climbed higher, past every place she wanted them to touch, until he wrenched her hands above her head.

She tried to lift her legs to rub against his inner thigh but he pinned her body to the bed with his legs and trapped her hands with one hand, while the other took a leisurely stroll across her body that short-circuited her senses. Kalilah would have been content to allow him to give her pleasure, but not this morning. There was no way she was going to let him touch her bare skin when she couldn't return the favor. She bucked against him, a feat that achieved little except to make her naked breasts sway at mouth level. He caught a nipple and bit softly before licking the pain away with a tongue slick with saliva.

Kalilah quickly abandoned the ineffective measures and focused instead on pressing against his impressive length, trapped between their bodies. It proved difficult at first but she arched up lightly before rubbing fiercely against him, his sharp intake of breath was a hard-won reward.

"Be quiet," he growled. She smiled.

"I haven't said a word," she pointed out in pure innocence.

"You will," he promised and returned to his explorations. His mouth blazed kisses along her exposed shoulder; he caught her long hair in his hand and pulled the kinky strands back to expose her throat fully to him. His breath fanned her all the way to the curve of her ears, and then he bent with an agonizing slowness so he could devour that, too.

He didn't need to hold her down anymore; anticipation and full-throttle desire was a stronger leash. All ideas of wanting to run her hands against his skin evaporated.

"Finn, please."

He did not pay mind to her words or the torment he was dealing – his measured pace continued and she breathed a sigh of relief when he trailed lower. Wet lips grazed against puckered nipple, but offered just a moment respite before it added to her hunger.

"Finn, please, I want you, please." Her words were delivered in a voice wracked by torturous aches without garnering a reaction from him. He merely tugged at the twin peaks, cupping her left breast with his large hands and sucked her. Her back arched impossibly off the bed. The force of it almost broke her mind, but he wasn't finished.

He swallowed, eyes completely trained at her face, enjoying her undoing without being moved as she pleaded with her eyes, voice temporarily lost.

And then he was kissing her again, but with tenderness, and not the jarring emotion of just moments before. His hands were everywhere, sweeping down her sides and back up, moving lower and then away from her secret place. She was drenched with desire and she couldn't even begin to plead with him. His mouth was dipping lower, to her collarbone, lower, finally, to the underside of her breast. She bucked beneath him again, mashing against his erection, but he was moving again before she could savor what he had done. He was above her, sweeping the hair from the sides of her face.

The thought would have startled her had she not been thinking about it all along, but there in that moment, it just seemed right. It just seemed like destiny that she was lying there in his arms.

Then without warning, he plunged into her. Her folds were drenched, slicking a smooth passage until he was buried deep within, but only for a moment. He pulled out until only his tip remained in her. She whimpered at the loss but he slammed back, driving her body forward with the force of his movement. She didn't care, not when she was bearing down on him.

The slow dance continued with calculated moves that left her dazed and just at the cusp of her orgasm, she chased it relentlessly, but he was not kind enough to just hand it to her. She tried to quicken the pace, but his hands held her waist, controlling her movement, restricting them.

She could have wept.

Her passage rippled against him in wet spasms; he clenched his jaw and Kalilah did it again, this time completely intentional. His hands curled against her skin and became claws that couldn't hold on hard enough, his measured strokes lost in a frenzy of movements, pounding in and out of her in a bid to slake their crazed desire. She bore down on him, her free hand raking his back in a private madness. When the climax hit her, she heard him call out her name, a far-away voice that couldn't begin to find her in the abyss she had tumbled into.

Her body writhed uncontrollably and then exploded into charged pieces that rivaled a supernova in its heat. Right before she poured past pure bliss, it occurred to her that they still hadn't used any protection during any of their escapades. *Shit!*

Finn closed the door of his office with a small smile on his face. A smile that an hour of haggling with marketing on the best form of advertising couldn't break. There was only one person responsible for that smile and he had to admit she was his drug.

Last night had blown his mind and body, but this morning it reminded him of what he was fighting for.

"Are you sure this is what you want to do?" His lawyer, Michelle, was seated on the plush sofa in his office.

"I'm sure. Is everything in order?"

"It just needs your signature."

"Perfect." He collected the proffered paper, one glance at the heading and he felt the indecision gripping him again but he could not live like that forever.

"Wait, are you absolutely sure about this?" The lawyer looked at his employer with worried eyes. In her opinion, the man looked too much at ease considering what he was about to do. "There are going to be strong repercussions."

"I hope so," Finn replied as he signed the papers and handed them back. "Did you get the other papers? I'd like to have them sent along with this one."

"I don't understand why you have to..." but Finn cut off the words with one look.

"It's not for you to understand." Finn reiterated and walked toward his view, "just do as I've told you." He was taking a leap of faith and hope that it all worked in his favor.

"I hope these papers bring you the fulfillment you rightly deserve. I apologize for everything that has happened in the past. You deserve a life that is lived on your own terms.

The tears rolled down her face with her completely oblivious to their existence. He had given her the annulment she had wanted. A gift; that was what he intended it to be. She was not going to accept it – not now, not ever – especially after the news she'd received earlier.

She reached for the second envelope and was shocked to see the deed to a building. It was the building where she had wanted to open her own organization. She was shocked. He gave her everything she had wanted and without even making a single demand on her. Setting her free to do exactly as she pleased. And she loved him for it but she couldn't accept none of it if he wasn't a part of it.

She would live the life she always wanted; one untainted by her parents and their expectations. A life she was robbed of by her own naivety and fears. The thought galvanized her into action; she left the papers on the table and raced to her room. She had a million and one things to do, starting with Finn first.

Forty-five minutes later after finding out from Finn's assistance where he was, she was running out of the door.

"How soon are you going to finish all those renovations and get the building in perfect working order?" Finn asked the short man who turned around in a slow circle to survey the building before returning to his starting point.

"With full crew working 12- to 16-hour shifts, six months at the very least," was his verdict.

"Can't it be done sooner?" He wanted the work done as soon as possible; six months seemed like a long time suddenly.

"I'm being very optimistic here, sir."

"Fine, how soon can you start renovations?"

The contractor turned another slow circle and Finn felt himself lose some more of his precious calm.

"As soon as we get the necessary municipal permits," he had not missed the impatience the man beside him radiated.

"Good, I've already applied for them and we should receive them soon." The rest of his words drowned out in the sound of the door being opened.

***

As if sensing her presence, a sudden shift in the air that only came when he was near her or when she was around him, Finn turned around with a rather gratifying smile on his face. She walked further into the room, transfixed with the picture in front of her. Finn, with another man beside him in her building, but she had eyes for him alone.

Finn turned to shake the man's hand and said, "Thanks a lot, I'll make sure the keys and permits are forwarded to your office by the end of the week."

"Of course. I look forward to working with you," the stranger replied before walking past her and nodded his greeting at her before he continued out the door. Finn stopped in front of her looking concerned. She saw the uncertainty.

"Hey, fancy meeting you here." Kalilah said.

"Broken down houses are the current rage."

"What are you doing here Finn?" Her brows furrowed at his flippant air.

"Just having a contractor work on your building," he replied easily as if it was the only obvious answer.

"Contractor?"

"There's quite a few renovations to be done before you can put it to use," he said in a matter-of-fact tone.

"I got the annulment papers. Why are you doing this?" There lay the crux of the matter.

"To answer your question, I'm doing this because I want to make things easier for you," he replied as if it was logical at all.

"After spending the past few days with you, you think signing the annulment papers would be easy for me?" Kalilah stuffed her fist into her mouth to stop her sobs but he caught her hands and tilted her face to catch the tears streaming down her face.

"Don't cry, babe."

She only cried harder.

"I'm sorry, I've been a fool. I thought I could do it. I thought I could force myself to give you what you wanted but I can't. I don't know what that makes me but I just want you to know I can't. Life without you isn't worth living but being with you knowing that you felt trapped into marrying me doesn't make me feel good. I love you too much to not give you the choice. I love you too much to keep you in a marriage that you're not sure you want to be in."

Kalilah cried louder at his admission, heart wrenching sobs that drove him to close the gap between them. His hands stroked her as he did that first night over five years ago when they shared their first kiss.

"Finn, I..." The words evaporated her tears as she tried to cut in but he stopped her.

"No, allow me to get this off my chest. I need to say this now. I fell in love with you five years ago, the somber daughter of Richard Anderson." She was surprised at his admission. "I know we dated, but it was for more than just companionship on my part. I knew you were younger than me, less experienced in life than me, but I wanted to spend the rest of my life with you from the moment I comforted you in that gazebo. And believe me when I say this, I would never have married you if I didn't love you with all my heart. Your father's company is not enough compensation for something like that. I don't regret falling in love with you," he explained.

"I should have listened to you back then."

"Both of us could have done things differently. Your father's machinations and our own fears cost us five years." Finn chuckled bitterly at that junction.

"I love you too, Finn."

"Kalilah, don't..."

"Don't what?"

"Offer me your heart in pity."

She looked at him now, eyes melded in a look that nothing could break.

"All I've ever wanted was your love, because I have always loved you," she finally admitted to him.

"Thank God," he breathed and hauled her closer to him, his head buried in her neck and her heart beating a frenzy in her chest as his hands surrounded her. "I have you now and I'm not letting you go."

"I choose you Finn. I chose you a long time ago." He looked at her intently. "I couldn't bring myself to tell you earlier. I was afraid of my own feelings when it came to you. I was scared by how vulnerable it made me feel," she admitted.

He fumbled in his pocket and brought out a small black box and then plunged to his knee.

"Kalilah, marry me and make my life worth living."

She gasped.

"You kept it?" It was the ring he had presented her with years ago. She had left it behind when she fled the country.

He gave her a small nod.

Kalilah had eyes only for the man who was making all her dreams come true. Her hand stole to her stomach and she knew the answer to give.

"Yes, we will!"

"We?"

She looked shyly into his eyes and said, "I took a pregnancy test earlier. It was positive."

Finn wore a look of pure joy as he got to his feet and hugged her body to his, this time he was not afraid to unleash the intensity of his emotions. Her hands came around his shoulders and held fast.

"And I'm going to devote the rest of my life to making sure you're both happy," he replied.

"And I will do the same for you," she promised.

"I have you and our child, that's all I need." At that declaration his hand stole between them to caress her flat stomach.

"We'll always talk to our children and offer them hugs and kisses," she said as his hand tightening around her waist again.

"And no pushing them into roles they don't want to assume," he said.

"Everything alright?" Kalilah whirled at the interruption to find Owen at the door.

"Everything is fine, Owen. You have the next two days off, my husband will see me home," she replied with a smile and she caught Owen's as well.

He wished them a good night and then retreated to the car.

The kiss started light but soon gathered heat as hands ventured beneath clothing.

"Not here," he rasped, his voice hoarse with arousal.

"Why not?" She returned her lips to his. "I want you right here; this place is ours. Your gift to me. I always want to remember how you made love to me here on the day we decided to take charge of our marriage."

"It's an old complex, Lilah. The floor is the only horizontal surface available. Let me take you home and to our bed." All perfectly factual points but she wanted him now.

"No," she insisted as she nipped at his lips, hands under his jacket retreating to her own top to remove one button, then another. She saw his resolve waver and when she pulled the material off her shoulder, she knew she had him. They spent the next hour bringing each other to new heights.

***

Finn hummed happily, leaning over to steal kisses from Kalilah for the fifth time within the space of three minutes as she gently nudged his head away.

"Eyes on the road, Sir," she teased. "I want a huge wedding this time," she said, her apparent joy filling the moving vehicle.

"The first time around was small and impersonal; we have a lot to make up for," he agreed.

"Kaiya wants to know what plans we have for the wedding." Kalilah held up her phone to show off her chat with her sister. "She says anything less than magnanimous wouldn't work for her, and I agree." She wanted to show off their love to everyone.

Finn gave her hand a quick squeeze and returned his attention to the road.

"Anything you want, my love."

"I'll never tire of hearing that."

"That you have me completely in your grasp?" Finn chuckled as he sped down the road.

"No, that you love me," she replied with a wide smile.

"I love you. I'll never tire of telling you." He wanted to hold her in his arms and tell her again and again.

"I love you too," she replied.

"I'll never tire of hearing it either," he promised, his eyes abandoning the road to look into her shining eyes.

She looked away from him in surprise and fear; he turned to look at what had her so terrified. He never saw it. He only felt the impact of the crash down to his very bones, and the tinkle of shattered glass before the darkness claimed him. He could hear her screaming his name.

EPILOGUE

FINN HAD BARELY UNSTRAPPED HIS TWINS, Maximillian and Milania, from their car seats when they alighted in an explosion of energy and skipped into the building. Their parents' admonitions were barely heard as they raced through the door.

Finn raced to the other side of the car to help his heavily pregnant wife out of the car.

"They exhaust me even when I'm only looking at them." Owen was on vacation at the moment, so Finn was his family's chauffeur for the time being. Not that he minded.

Kalilah sighed as she placed her feet on the ground, one hand massaging the small of her back and another lazily caressing her swollen stomach.

"Trust your kids to make sure I never have a moment's rest."

"I love you." Finn smiled at her resigned expression, "and I'm sure you'll finally get some rest when the baby is here."

"Remember the birth of the twins?" she prompted. Finn shuddered in mock fear.

"But it will be one baby this time."

"Having one newborn should be easier than having two," she returned with a smile wider than his had been. "I love you, even though your children exhaust me."

"I know," he replied and reached behind her for her purse. He snagged her hand, leading her towards the dance studio.

Four years after their reunion, and after that fateful accident on the road, he had everything he wanted – if you could call a crazed psycho-ex-boyfriend crashing into them an 'accident'.

He didn't think it was, the law didn't either, and Jonathan had gone to prison for attempted murder and would soon be deported back to the US. He had suffered a broken leg and now had a limp from that accident, but Kalilah was thankfully unharmed and his babies were born healthy, exactly eight months later. That was all that mattered to him.

A few things had happened after the incident.

He and Kalilah lived with their children in a five-bedroom, lakefront house in the west of Montréal. Kalilah had accomplished her dream of opening her non-profit organization for women, and served as the director. Kalilah's father had semi-retired and Finn had assumed the role of CEO at Anderson Realty. Kaiya's dancing school was thriving, and stayed fully booked throughout the year with classes for young aspiring dancers.

Kalilah had forgiven her father, but she never forgot all he had done to her. The children were introduced to their grandparents, but emotions were strained during such events. Her mom, who had always been cold to her and Kaiya when they were growing up, was surprisingly warm and patient with her grandchildren, especially her grandson.

The biggest change that had happened was the relationship between Kalilah's parents. Kalilah's dad had moved out of their family estate, and no one knew the reason. Neither of his in-laws spoke about what caused the rift between them, and Finn wondered again what could have driven the couple apart.

But none of that truly mattered to him, not when he could see his wife, content and happy, and his two children – soon three – healthy balls of energy bouncing all over the place. He was so happy; they were so happy that not even the past could taint it. Not when they had the rest of their lives to look forward to. Choosing not to dwell on the sadness the past held, but rather linger in the joyful moment, he hurried after his wife and entered Kaiya's dance school to a rather wonderful sight of what he could only attest to be growth.

"Finn!" Jalissa waved at Finn and invited him over to the group who had arrived before them.

Kaiya came over with a warm hug for Finn, while Katherine kissed her grandchildren, who seemed really happy to see her. Kaiya then hoisted up the twins on each of her hips and headed to the back room of the dance studio.

"Katherine, I didn't expect to see you here," Finn said as he placed a kiss on each of her cheeks.

"I wouldn't miss the opportunity to see my grandchildren perform in their first talent show," Kalilah's mother replied.

The entrance door swung open his parents and siblings came in. He went over to greet his mom and siblings. They had come from Ottawa just to see the twins' dance performance and he was glad for it.

"I hope we're not late," said his mom.

"No, you're not, Mom, we only just got here ourselves."

Kalilah came over to greet his parents, and his mom placed her hand over Kalilah's stomach.

"Where are my munchkins?" his sister asked.

"Yes, where are my babies?" his mom asked.

"They're in the back with Kaiya," he replied. He could see his younger brother eyeing Jalissa, and he gave him a cool look. Justin only winked at him and made his way over to where Jalissa stood. Before he could intervene, the entrance door swung open again, prompting Finn to take note of a rather awkward stare from his wife, Katherine, and Jalissa towards the door.

"Can I speak to Kaiya Anderson?" A masculine voice spoke from behind Finn.

Jalissa and Katherine both looked stricken. Something in Katherine's eyes held something more; fear, maybe shame Finn surmised. Their reaction prompted Finn to turn around and look from the man and back to them and then back again.

"Tyler? What the hell are you doing here?" Finn heard Jalissa ask, anger evident in her voice.

Something about the man made the women nervous, and he could only wonder what exactly it was about his new partner that had them on edge. Something was amiss, and Finn seemed to be the only one who wasn't in the loop.

Before You Go...

I hope that you enjoyed Kalilah and Finn's story and will leave a review or rating on Amazon or Goodreads. I can't thank you enough for taking time out of your busy life to read my story. I want to show you my appreciation by doing a giveaway. I have two $15 Amazon gift cards up for grabs. All you have to do to win is:

Download a copy of Claiming His Wife. If you bought the book, screenshot the email or if you have kindle unlimited screenshot this page.

Like my Facebook author page: @NiomieRoland

Post your screenshot on my Facebook author page.

Or

Follow me on Instagram at Niomie Roland and DM me your screenshots for a chance to win.

Two winners will be chosen at random and they will be announced on December 21st, 2019 on my Facebook page.

Author's Notes

I never intended to write a book about Finn and Kalilah. I was writing Kaiya and Tyler's story when Kalilah's story kept popping up in my mind and refused to be ignored. I became intrigued by K & F and I finally decided to pause work on Kaiya's story and started writing Kalilah and Finn's. Writing this one was fun for me since I was excited to see where these two lovers would lead me, but it was also stressful. Kalilah kept going back and forth with her feelings and I became frustrated throughout the process, however I never gave up. In the end I have to say that I am happy that they got their second chance. I hope you enjoyed their story as much as I did and look forward to reading Kaiya and Tyler's story soon.

Love Always,
Niomie

Ps: Keep swiping for the preview of my other title "My Wife's Baby."

BEFORE BRAD CAME HOME...

HIS MESSAGE CAME IN AT EXACTLY 7:00AM, when Alana was lying on the bed rubbing her finger against the sensitive area where her wisdom tooth used to be. When the phone pinged she picked it up and smiled when his name showed up.

She was still on his mind.

The message read: You looked beautiful today at the super market.

It was puzzling. He was supposed to be in the UK, not anywhere near the supermarket she visited to get groceries from this evening. How did he see her? Her brow was furrowed in puzzlement as she typed a reply.

I looked… wait, are you in town?

A fresh message from him popped in almost immediately, just as she was about to place the phone on her nightstand to go and check up on Aaryn. She grimaced as she felt a numb pain in her private area. "Must have moved too quickly or something," she mused. She got up from the bed and walked out of the room to the nursery. The house seemed empty without her husband. It was a two storied townhouse with three big bedrooms and only two ladies in it presently; two ladies who were desperately missing the only man in their lives.

Right now, however, her husband Brad was the furthest thing from Alana's mind. She stood at the door and watched her daughter sleep. Aaryn was lying on her side with her teddy bear clutched in her plump hands.

Alana padded to her bed and kissed her softly on the cheek. Then she turned and hurried out of the room. When she got back to her room she picked up the stack of laundry that was lying at the foot of her bed and walked to her closet. When she was done situating all of the clothes, she noticed that her appearance came into view of the full length mirror that hung on the closet door. Her thick curly hair laid in a bun on top of her head. A few tendrils of hair fell around her round face. Her caramel skin showcased her smooth, clear complexion. Thank God.

During her teenage years her face was plagued by acne and pimples. She tried every remedy possible to achieve the lustrous skin she was now admiring. She was medium height and 130lbs the last time she weighed herself. She turned her body slightly to study herself from the back. Yep; curved in all the right places. After studying herself she walked over to the nightstand, picked up her phone, her hand shaking with excitement, and plopped back onto the bed.

Greg's message was waiting for her on her phone screen: Yeah baby.

It brought a smile to her face and she typed a quick reply: Wow!

It was like he was waiting for her. He continued their quick exchange. From then on, the chat flew smoothly.

The same thing I said to myself when I saw you.

She smirked. Oh yeah? Lol.

Oh yeah. I said even more, but I don't believe they are things you've never heard.

She paused and readjusted her position on the bed. Lol. Flatterer.

We have to meet up.

Her eyebrow raised. Meet up?

Yeah. Since I saw you today, I have been dying to see you again.

When did you get back?

Yesterday. Damn. London is shit.

How long are you staying?

Forever. Dan wants me here.

Dan, Greg's older brother, was poised to take over their late father's position as principal partner at Sheffield, Barber and Carlson, one of the biggest law firms in the country. It appeared that he wanted Greg beside him as he was wary of going against the sharks who owned the firm with his father before the old man died.

Okay, great.

So, when are you coming over? I've got my place all prepped up already in anticipation of your arrival.

Persistent, are we? She chuckled to herself, then responded. Lol. Greg, I'm not coming to your place.

Why? All that effort, Jesus.

Come on, Greg. What would we do at your place?

Drink, talk, catch up on old times.

Hmm, she considered it for a few moments, then another text came through.

Look, I'll totally lose it if I don't see you this weekend.

She sighed. Okay-okay-okay. But not your place.

He shot back immediately. Why?

Brad's face briefly flashed across her mind. Never mind. Where and what time?

Her phone pinged with another message after she finished with Greg. This one was from her dentist, Dr. Fred Luther. He had extracted her tooth in his clinic, and he wanted to know if she was okay.

How is the patient doing?

Almost as soon as she read that text, she felt more discomfort in her private area. I must have pulled something during my workout. She shot back a quick reply, hoping Fred wouldn't want to have a long, drawn out conversation with her too.

I'm okay Fred.

Fred was one of her husband's frat brothers from their college days.

You won't forget your appointment next week, right?

She rolled her eyes and lifted her finger to reply to Fred, but another message from Greg popped in and she scrolled up to view it.

It was a kissing emoji.

It amused her, but she sent one back. Anything to keep his daydream going.

1

STORM CLOUDS WERE AMASSING IN THE EAST. They looked angry enough to flood an entire city, but they were nothing compared to the clouds hanging over Brad Johnson's head.

Even though he was driving, his best friend Cliff noticed it. As he maneuvered the car through the heavy traffic on Fifth Street, he stole a glance at his friend from time to time.

Brad had just won the Associate of the Year award for the third time running. On nights like this, he was always noisy, talking about everything on earth while cradling his champagne. But tonight, his bottle of champagne lay on the back seat, beside his briefcase and his award plaque.

His lips were sealed, and his handsome face was creased by a frown. That frown had been there since the night began. Not even the presentation of the award and the wide smiles of the managing partner as he handed it to him earlier that night had been enough to drive it away. His mind had been far away from the hotel where the law firm held the award dinner.

It had been on the woman who had bailed on him at the last minute because of a headache: Alana, his wife.

"Are you okay?" Cliff asked.

"Yea, I am," Brad answered. "Why?"

"You look like a man whose wife ran away with some other man."

That statement made Brad go cold. It was the last thing Cliff should have said.

"What the fuck do you mean?"

"What do you mean, what the fuck do I mean?"

Cliff's surprise was written all over his face. His bushy eyebrows were raised and his wide mouth was open.

"Hey, watch the road!"

Cliff turned in time to see that he was about to veer off the road onto the sidewalk. Hastily he swung the steering wheel left, bringing the car back into their lane. "Jesus Christ!"

Brad shook his head in wonder. "One of these days you will get us killed!"

"You distracted me, man."

"I dis…," Brad looked at Cliff in disbelief. "Just shut up and drive. Only God knows how the hell you were able to get a driving license."

"Shut up dude."

"I will if you do the same."

"I won't have you saying nonsense about my driving."

"I'll stop, when you stop driving like a drunk!"

Cliff turned to glare at him and he pointed at the road. The mouth that had opened to fire a retort closed and Cliff turned his attention back to the road muttering obscenities under his breath.

"I want to return home to my wife in one piece," Brad said.

"Keep talking and you may return to her in countless pieces."

Brad began to laugh and Cliff joined him. But the laughter didn't last long. He wasn't eager to return home to Alana. He was in Cliff's car, going home because he didn't know where else to go after the award dinner. Going home now meant having to make a decision he didn't want to make yet. It was one he had never thought he would be faced with.

Alana's ex was in town. That alone was not enough to worry him. The man was past tense, and Brad was the only love of her life now. Or, at least he was supposed to be. But the problem was that Alana had been acting strange lately. Worse still, Brad knew that she had seen her ex at least twice since he returned to town. But she hadn't told him. So he was worried. He was so worried that he wanted to ask her what was going on. But another part of him was telling him that there was nothing going on.

For a week now, his head had been more mired in confusion than the people who tried to erect the Tower of Babel. It was a surprise that he had even managed to get anything done at the office at all. It was the fact that there were bills to be paid that kept him moving.

He didn't know when the car left Fifth Street. He also didn't know when they got to his street and rolled to a stop before his house. His mind was in the middle of an intense debate session. To confront her, or not. That was the bone of contention between the two sides; those lingering voices of reason which made indecision a living, breathing thing.

It was Cliff's voice that snapped him out of his reverie. "Dude!"

It startled him because it was loud.

"Where did you go to?" Cliff asked.

Brad was confused. "Where did I-when?"

"I called you like a million times."

"A million times?"

"Look, I don't know what's bugging you, but you have to deal with it, okay?"

"Nothing's bugging me."

Cliff placed a hand on his shoulder. It was big, like everything about Cliff. Cliff was six feet five inches of muscle with eyes that could take in the entire planet in one glance, a nose that could inhale enough air to fill a gas tank at one go and a mouth that could take off another man's head in one bite if cannibalism suddenly appealed to him; the perfect physique for the notorious courtroom brawler.

"You have been moody since you came back and I don't like it," he said.

"I'm okay," Brad insisted.

"Whatever. Just bear one thing in mind."

"What's that?"

"Whenever you decide to unburden, just know that I am here for you. Daddy's got you, baby."

For a moment Brad stared at him with a poker face, then he nodded almost imperceptibly. "Goodnight Cliff."

He grabbed his things from the back seat and opened his door quickly.

When he got out of the car, he didn't stand to wave and watch Cliff drive away like he always did. Instead he turned and made his way up the short drive with quick steps. His gleaming black shoes made a crunch-crunch sound as he walked.

When he reached the front door he stopped and took a deep breath. To confront her, or not?

The door swung open suddenly and she emerged; Alana, the love of his life. Brad could not understand why she looked more beautiful than she had ever looked at that moment. The smile on her face warmed his insides. The warmth started out from the pit of his stomach and spread up to his heart, his arms and then his face. His face broke into a smile.

"Baby…"

He placed his brief case and the champagne on the floor and spread his arms. Smiling, she walked into them. In that moment, when her bosom pressed into his chest, his mind was wiped clean. All the thoughts that had been tormenting him fled.

2

ALANA'S SKIN WAS THAT PERFECT SHADE OF CARAMEL that could effortlessly turn heads. It glowed and was also flawless. It was that skin that had drawn Brad to her in the first place. When he drew closer, her beautiful brown eyes had captivated him.

Theirs had been love at first sight. It had been a chance meeting in their college days. The clichéd, bumping into each other in the library with her books falling from her hands and him bending to get them for her.

The only words that had been spoken were two hasty "sorrys" proffered by both parties with apologetic smiles on their faces. They had gone on their separate ways, but fate conspired and brought them back together again in a Black Lives Matter rally.

Being a man who understood the times and seasons, Brad took this second meeting as a sign from the cosmos and chatted her up after the rally. She had initially been surprised to see him – a white man – at the rally, but her shock quickly subsided as they grew more comfortable with each other. She saw how compassionate, kind and thoughtful he was to others, especially her. Besides, there were other white people who attended the rally as well.

Although it was the first time Brad and Alana had a full conversation, they spent over two hours in the café where they had gone for coffee and books. A date followed a few days later after hours of phone conversations and texting. More dates, phone calls and texts followed that date, until the two ended up at the altar putting rings on each other's fingers. It was inevitable. Alana would later admit that Brad's integrity, confidence and greyish-blue eyes made falling in love with him easy.

Now, as they held each other in a tight embrace Brad marveled at how lucky he was. This woman was someone who understood him, supported him and loved him fiercely, despite his many imperfections. Sometimes he even doubted if he loved her as much as she did him.

"I'm sorry," Alana said.

Brad held her back to have a look at her face. There was a wan smile there. "For what?" he asked her.

"I should have been at the party with you," she said almost in a whisper.

"It's okay baby. You had a headache."

"But I should have still managed it."

"For what? So old Roger could drool all over you and get his wife jealous again?"

Brad forced out a laugh. Alana didn't join him. She didn't find his joke funny. Last year, the managing partner, Roger Sandler had bumped into one of the waitresses while staring at her derriere, much to the ire of his wife.

"It was boring really."

"Someone brought the champagne home again." Alana clapped her hands in delight and bent to get the briefcase and the champagne off the floor.

"Yeah baby." The smile on Brad's face had a hint of pride in it.

"The third time," Alana stood on tiptoes and kissed him on the lips, "Baby you are just the best!"

"You can say that again."

"You are the best."

Brad nodded and gave her smoldering kiss.

"Do you want to hear it again?" She asked almost breathlessly.

"Just one more time please."

"You are the best goddamn lawyer in this town!"

"Thank you for saying that," he responded while kissing her lips and placing a trail of kisses that led to her delicate neck.

Alana led the way as they walked across the living room to the staircase. Brad ran his hand over the sofa closest to him as he walked behind his wife, thinking of all the things they'd do tonight in the privacy of their bedroom. He was getting excited just thinking about it.

"Is Aaryn in bed?" he asked her.

"Yeah. I tucked her in earlier; she missed you," Alana replied.

"She didn't miss me too much, did she?"

"She asked for her daddy every minute."

"Aww, I missed my baby as well."

"I told her you would be the first face she would see in the morning."

Okay, now that that was out of the way, maybe they could start something. Brad hastened his steps and caught up with her just as her right foot settled on the first step. He was about to grab her waist when her cell phone began to ring.

"Who could that be?" Brad felt his lust fade when he considered that it was after 11:00pm. Alana had a puzzled look on her face when she turned. "Go on upstairs and take your shower; I'll be waiting for you in the kitchen."

She raised the champagne bottle and gave him a wink.

***

She was still on the phone when Brad came downstairs twenty minutes later. He had taken his shower and kissed their daughter goodnight before going to the kitchen. Aaryn was already fast asleep when he tiptoed into her room, but that didn't matter. It was a tradition he kept whenever he was home.

She was a carbon copy of her mother. Light brown eyes that were hidden by her eyelids as she slept and long eyelashes that swept her cheeks. A head full of black hair like her mother's and cheeks that dimpled when she smiled. It was her skin that betrayed the paternity of her parents. It was that lighter shade of brown that most biracial kids of parents of mixed races have.

They had her in the second year of their marriage. An unplanned kid that had marred their plans to enjoy each other for five years before letting any children into their lives. Her coming was funny because they should have known better. There were better and more trusted ways they could have used to keep their marriage to themselves, but they had chosen coitus interruptus of all things. Perhaps this was why

Brad had forgiven Aaryn for coming when she did and had fallen in love with her, almost as quickly as he did her mother.

"I love you," he whispered and kissed her cheek. After, he remained bent over her, listening to her breathe, then he turned and padded out.

His steps on the staircase were lighter than they had been when he had gone up. Alana's headache was probably gone now, so if he wanted to start something in the kitchen, the coast would be clear. It was easy to reach the conclusion that her headache had come from her intense dislike of his law firm, Sandler, Harris and Whistler.

That dislike had stemmed from the fact that there was no love lost between him and the partners in the firm. Brad was the reason. He was the mule, the beast of burden who did all the heavy lifting and they were the big mouths who ate all the proceeds from his labor.

It was just a word of this in her ears that had been enough to paint the firm black in her eyes. Now, all she wanted was for him to get the hell out of that place. His yearning for a strictly corporate firm did not help matters. All she did these days was beg him to open his own practice or find a new employer.

Alana was in the kitchen when he came down. Her voice floated to his ears as he crossed the living room. She was laughing hard. When he entered the kitchen, he saw her on a stool with her cell phone pressed to her ears.

He stood by the doorway for a while watching her, wondering who she was talking to. Slowly, the fears he had left outside the house when she opened the door to let him in started to come back. They came back in waves, each higher than the other, threatening to drown him.

At first, he tried to guess who she was talking to.

It was easy to eliminate her mother and her sister. Those two did not know how to laugh. They needed people like Alana to make them laugh.

It was also easy to eliminate her friends. Tasha and Willa were fun people, but this was not the kind of laughter that originated from them. It was the crazy thigh slapping, foot stomping laughter that resulted from hearing juicy bits of gossip that were also funny.

No. This laughter was different. It was a…

Brad turned and went back to the living room to wait. While waiting he tried not to think about Alana and her phone call. He settled on one of the sofas and leaned back, closing his eyes with a sigh. They were arranged in a U form, with a long sofa at the base and two love seats at the sides. Behind them, a book case and a giant vase of flower stood. It was Alana's arrangement, something that had been done in one of those moments when interior design had caught her fancy.

Brad could still remember her breathless laughter when she showed him her handiwork. It sounded almost the same as the one coming from the kitchen now. Lord, it grated on his nerves. Why was she keeping him waiting? Who was so important that she had to put their plans on hold?

Suddenly an urge to creep to the kitchen door and eavesdrop came upon him. Resisting it was harder than Brad thought it would be. It was something that people with insecurity issues did. He was not that kind of person. He could not be that kind of person now.

Unfortunately, despite Brad's notions of being above the insecurities of common men, the urge did not die down. It only got stronger. It attacked him like a ferocious boxer eager to get his weakened opponent down to the canvas.

When he couldn't hold in his curiosity anymore, he got up and went back up the stairs. When he got to the master bedroom, he looked at the time on the clock and saw that he had been waiting for ten minutes. Alana had been on the phone with Mr. Funny for thirty minutes.

To read the remainder of this title, go to Amazon and search the title "My Wife's Baby" by Niomie Roland.

$10.99

Made in the USA
Middletown, DE
24 April 2023